THE CASEBOOK

OF

ABEE NORMAL

PARANORMAL INVESTIGATIONS

VOLUME 2

CLAUDIA HALL CHRISTIAN

ALSO BY CLAUDIA HALL CHRISTIAN
STORIESBYCLAUDIA.COM

ABEE NORMAL, PARANORMAL INVESTIGATIONS
The Casebook of Abee Normal, Paranormal Investigations, Volume 1
The Casebook of Abee Normal, Paranormal Investigations, Volume 2

THE DENVER CEREAL

The Denver Cereal	Fort Lupton
Celia's Puppies	Fort Morgan
Cascade	Fort Collins
Cimarron	Olney Springs
Black Forest	Manitou Springs
Fairplay	Idaho Springs
Gold Hill	Poncha Springs
Silt	Hot Sulfur Springs
Larkspur	Glenwood Springs (5/19)
Firestone	Pagosa Springs (2019)

Grand Junction (Denver Cereal V1-10)
Fort Garland (Denver Cereal V11-13)

ALEX THE FEY THRILLERS
The Fey
Learning to Stand
Who I am
Lean on Me
In the Grey
Finding North
About Face
In Deep (2019)

THE QUEEN OF COOL
The Queen of Cool

SETH AND AVA MYSTERIES
Tax Assassin
Carving Knife
Friendly Fire
Cigarette Killer
Little Girl Blue (May 2019)

SUFFER A WITCH
Suffer a Witch

PUBLISHER'S NOTE:

This is a work of fiction. Names, characters, places and incidents either are either the product of the author's imagination or are used fictitiously.

Cover by Amanda Walker

Casebook Volume 02 © May 2019

Cook Street Publishing, LLC
ISNI: 0000 0004 1443 6403
PO Box 7247
Denver, CO 80207

SEVEN

The case of:
The Bogle's Warning

It was late when Abee heard Everett take the stairs two at a time. He arrived at the bathroom on the third floor and closed the door. She was sitting with her hand on his twin, Emily's, back. Emily was lying on her side with her back to Abee. Emily's body was wrapped around Abee's Plott Hound, Goji. Jeremiah was asleep in an armchair near the bed.

When Everett left the bathroom, Abee leaned over to kiss Emily's cheek. Emily opened her eyes.

"My sister," Emily said. "Forever."

Grinning, Emily fell back to sleep. Abee got up. Goji lifted her head from the bed to see if Abee wanted the dog to go with her. Abee shook her head and gestured with her hand for Goji to lie back down. The dog's head dropped to the bed. Jeremiah opened his eyes when Abee opened the door. Abee smiled, and he nodded.

Jeremiah would stay with Emily in Abby's safe, familiar room.

Abee ducked into the bathroom before going to where Everett was waiting for her in the guest bedroom across from Abee's room on the third floor of Ma'am's house. Tonight was Abee and Everett's wedding night. At the door, Abee sighed.

All of her girlish dreams of wedding nights had evaporated when Everett and Emily's father had hung himself. Abee's own mother, Joanna, had been found at the bottom of the long marble stairwell below Emery's hanging body. Emily had had a front-row seat to everything that had transpired.

At the time, Everett and Abee had been in Connecticut, getting married. They, Abee and Everett's best friend, Penelope "Pen" Calamus, Abee's Ma'am, and Abee's lawyer Jason Fremont had piled onto a small plane, which landed at the county airport. As soon as they landed, Abee had gone to the hospital to see her mother, while Everett had gone with Ma'am, Pen, and Abee's lawyer to deal with the mess his father had created.

Abee closed her eyes. This was the first time she'd seen Everett alone since she had lost her mind over a Bogle while visiting him in New Jersey, where he was going to Princeton. The Bogle mirrored to Abee her deepest fear — that she would lose Everett. While Abee thought she was afraid of losing Everett to someone whiter and wealthier, her great-or-something-like-that grandmother Ma'am thought that Abee knew that she would outlive him.

Abee opened the door. Everett looked up the moment the door opened. He was sitting on the bed in his wedding tuxedo. He pulled a Hostess Twinkie out of his pocket.

"Wedding cake," Everett said. He pulled a can of Fanta Orange from his pants pocket. "Champagne to toast the bride."

Abee grinned at his efforts, and he laughed. He set the dessert cake and the can of orange drink down on the desk next to the bed and went to her. Taking her hand, he led her to her sewing table. He sat her down in a chair, and he grabbed the chair from the desk. He brought the "wedding cake" and "champagne" to the sewing table.

Silently, they pantomimed traditional wedding festivities. He held the Twinkie up for her to take a bite. She took a bite and chewed. After she swallowed, she held the Twinkie up for him. He took a bite. They grinned at each other. They passed the dessert cake between them two more times, each bite getting ever smaller, until Everett finished it.

Abee jumped up. Opening the closet, she pulled a large plastic bag from the shelf in the closet. She dug through paper plates and napkins, until she found red plastic cups. She gave one to Everett and took another for herself. Everett poured the orange drink into their cups.

Linking elbows, they drank the sweet orange drink. When they finished, he leaned forward and they kissed.

"Do you regret . . .?" he started.

"No," she said. "You?"

"No way," he said with a sigh. "I *do* regret all the rest of this crap."

He shook his head. He tugged at his bow tie.

"How is Emily?" Everett asked of his twin.

Emily had Down Syndrome. Abee and Everett had met when his father had hired Abee to tutor Emily. Abee loved Emily almost as much as Everett.

"Good," Abee said. "Better, really. Did you see her face when you told her about us?"

"I've never seen her happier," Everett said.

"She kept saying, 'You're my sister forever now,'" Abee said with a smile.

"'You're the fox?'" Everett repeated what Emily had said to him.

Everett and Abee had dated in secret because Emery had threatened to throw Everett and Emily out of the house if Everett dated an African-American. This didn't stop them. They even went to prom dressed in costumes — Everett went dressed as a fox, and Abee went dressed as a crow.

"That was a really great moment," Everett said. "You sure you . . .?"

"I'm sure," Abee said. "Ma'am brought some T-shirts up here for us. You saw the toothbrush?"

Everett nodded. Abee gestured to two clean T-shirts on top of the desk before going to open the windows.

"It's stuffy in here," Abee said.

Everett silently changed from his wedding tuxedo into the white cotton T-shirt. He sat down on the bed. The cool night breeze came off the tall evergreens which surrounded the house. The stuffy warm room soon smelled of fresh forest pine. The light of a waning moon and the stars shone through the ancient windows. Abee turned her back to him and sat down at the sewing table to slip off her hose. Ever the Southern gentleman, Everett gave her the space she needed to undress.

Abee looked around for Tippi, her ever-present Sprite, to help her with her zipper before remembering that she had sent Tippi home to see her family. Abee tried the zipper of her peach lace dress, but the zipper stuck.

"Let me," Everett said.

He gently tugged the fabric away from the zipper and unzipped the dress before retreating to the other side of the room. While she changed, he plugged his cell phone into a pair of speakers on the desk. Muddy Waters came from the speakers. Abee sighed as her personal Bogle shut up for the first time since they'd arrived home. Abee quickly changed into her white T-shirt. When she turned around, he was lying on the queen bed in his boxer briefs and a white T-shirt. She sat down on the bed.

"Do you want to talk about it?" Abee asked.

CASEBOOK VOLUME 02,
Abee Normal, Paranormal Investigations   6
The case of the Bogle's Warming

"No," Everett said. He stroked her cheek. "But I think we should."

"Why should we?" Abee asked.

"Because it's likely that Beauchamp family hell will descend in the morning," Everett said. His family name was Beauchamp.

"What do you mean?" Abee asked.

"Oh," Everett sighed. "I can tell you about it later. First, I want to know how you are. Please. Talk to me."

"I'm sad," Abee said. "Confused."

"About us?" Everett asked, his insecurity flaring up.

"About everything else," Abee said shaking her head.

"Me, too," Everett said with a nod. "How is your mother?"

Abee's mother's multiple sclerosis had been in remission. She'd been relatively well when she'd taken up her relationship with Everett's father again.

"Oh," Abee said with a sigh. "Alive. I guess. She has a broken leg and elbow from the fall. 'Nothing that won't heal.' That's what the doctor says. I just don't know how she'll be when she wakes up and hears that Emery is dead."

"But she will wake up," Everett said.

"The doctors are optimistic," Abee said. "They say that she was severely dehydrated and her electrolytes were off."

"The electricity is off in the house," Everett said. "The pumps to the well would have stopped working."

"They had no water," Abee said. "God, how awful."

Everett nodded.

"Did Dad push her down the stairs?" Everett asked.

"No one will ever know," Abee said. "Or, I should say, no one living knows. Emery fired the house staff weeks ago. The three of them were there alone. Until I have a chance to ask the ghosts what happened, I think we can safely assume that she fell. The doctor said that. in her condition, it was possible that she fell. Not probable, but possible."

Abee put her hand on his chest.

"Emery never physically injured Joanna," Abee said.

"Just emotionally gutted her a time or two," Everett said.

Abee gave him a sad nod.

"They were so entwined," Abee said. She sighed and looked away. "The doctor said that Joanna had been really lucky to be so well for such a long period of time. It's likely that she'll deteriorate quickly now. Or that's what he said."

Abee looked out the open windows at the trees and the stars beyond.

"He said that we should brace ourselves for her steep decline," Abee said. She sucked in her breath in a kind of sob. "I'm sure that she kept herself alive on the off chance that Emery would love her again. And now . . ."

Silent tears rolled down Abee's face.

"What does Ma'am say?" Everett asked quickly.

"What she said before," Abee said.

Together they said, "'It's up to Joanna now.'"

"I . . ." Abee said. She nodded before speaking in a rush of words. "The child in me wants *my* Mommy to fight this thing . . . to live until old age . . . to be happy and find real, true, healthy love. But my heart keeps telling me that she will slip away the moment she learns that Emery is dead. Certainly I've never been enough for her to live for. She's been so sick . . . so sick. How can I ask her to endure enormous pain and infirmity for . . .? She's always fought on for . . ."

Overwhelmed with sorrow, Abee fell silent as she cried.

"It's always been my dad," Everett said.

Abee nodded. She wiped her moist face with an edge of the T-shirt and took a breath. Turning to him, she scanned his face.

"How are you?" Abee asked.

"I'm . . ." Everett said. After a moment, he sighed. "I knew this would happen. I mean, I didn't know dad would kill himself or that he would do that to Em, I knew that all of his financial crap would blow up in my face, our faces and . . ."

Everett fell silent.

"And?" Abee asked.

"Every fucking thing revolves around that stupid plantation," Everett said.

"Everything?" Abee asked.

Everett's eyes scanned her face. He let out another sigh.

"According to the original deed of the plantation, the land and the house are to stay in the family," Everett said.

"Because of your grandfather?" Abee asked.

"Because of everything," Everett said. "From the original land grant that was renewed after the Civil War was over. The formation documents."

"What happens if it doesn't stay in Beauchamp hands?" Abee asked.

"There isn't an 'if' there," Everett said. "Emery should not have been able to borrow against the land. Period. But he did. The banks can't foreclose on the land, which, I'm sure, is why he borrowed against the plantation. Slimy bastard never had any intention of paying the money back. He just never considered, that by borrowing the money, he became vulnerable to the other branches of the family, other Beauchamps."

Abee scowled.

"Tomorrow morning, there will be a hoard of Beauchamp descendants looking for their piece of the plantation," Everett said. "But the plantation can't be split up. It can't be cut into sections. It has to remain whole and complete or cease to exist altogether."

"We can't sell off the fields?" Abee asked.

"As far as I can tell, no one knows," Everett said. "That's just how it's set up."

Abee nodded and vowed to ask Ma'am in the morning.

"My great-grandfather cut his other children out of the will, right?" Everett asked. "And my dad took the plantation and all inheritance away from his sister and brother, right?"

Abee nodded.

"Turns out that's in the charter, too," Everett said. "'Only the eldest Beauchamp male shall take possession of the house and lands.'"

"Lucky you," Abee said.

"Well, now the oldest male is Ted," Everett said. "Not me. Ted. Rules of dynasties."

"But your grandfather's brothers and sisters . . ." Abee started.

"That's because my dad was able to keep his father's death a secret until he owned the plantation outright,"

Everett said. "I can't really do that when Dad's death is on the nightly national news."

"The national news?" Abee winced.

Everett nodded.

"Why?" Abee asked. She added immediately, "Wait! I don't care. Please, go on."

Everett looked at her for a moment before continuing.

"Dad's suicide puts everything on hold for at least six weeks," Everett said. "The local probate judge is a friend of his, so it could be eight weeks or . . ."

Everett shrugged.

"I think I know what you're saying, but . . ." Abee said.

"He killed himself so that I would have more time to come up with money to save the plantation," Everett said. "Or to pressure you into giving me the money or . . ."

"He killed himself for the plantation," Abee said.

"He lived for the plantation," Everett said. "He gave up everything in his life for that stupid plantation. I'm sure that he gave up his life for it."

Abee put her hand over his heart. She knew how much this hurt Everett. For a long moment, their eyes held.

"You're angry," Abee said.

"I'm exhausted," Everett said. "All of this is so . . . wrong. So wrong. Who kills themself to force their son to find financing for some stupid, falling-down house and fields that don't grow anything?"

"Do you think he was being hounded by . . ." Abee started.

"Elaine?" Everett asked. "Yes. She was at the plantation when we got there. Not your Bogle. The flesh-and-blood woman. She wanted to know when she was going to get control of the estate."

"Can she do that?" Abee asked.

"Not now," Everett said. "Now that Dad has killed himself, everything is on hold."

Everett looked off into space. He sniffed and looked at Abee.

"Mom called," Everett said.

"Oh?" Abee asked.

"She didn't ask about me or Em or how we were or . . . I mean, I got married today, and . . ."

Everett's heart broke and tears began to fall down his face.

"She wants to know when she gets her . . . her . . . share. 'I've been patient, Everett, but the divorce is settled, and I am due my share.'"

Everett covered his eyes with his hand. Abee kept her hand over Everett's heart until he gained control over his emotions.

"I'm sorry," Everett said.

"Don't be," Abee said. "This stuff . . . all of it . . . it's heartbreaking."

He held out his arms, and Abee got into the bed next to him. She laid her head on his shoulder, and he scooted her close.

"This feels . . ." Everett said.

"Like we're going to get caught," Abee said with a laugh.

Everett laughed.

"Great," Everett said. "I was going to say 'great.' You are the single best thing that's ever happened to me."

Abee kissed his lips.

"Where's Pen?" Everett asked.

"She's just below us," Abee said. "My lawyer's in the other small bedroom below us. He agrees with you. He thinks tomorrow is going to be a doozy of a day."

"Did I tell you that my grandfather had a mistress?" Everett asked. "She and their children were in his will, too. Emery screwed her like he screwed everyone else."

"How?" Abee asked.

"No one of African blood can inherit," Everett said.

"He should have checked his own damned blood," Abee said.

Everett kissed the top of her head.

"We're going to break it all, aren't we?" Everett asked. "Make it new."

"Make it right," Abee said. "Make it new."

"Make it right," Everett said.

She lay with the back of her head against his shoulder for a moment before turning into him. She opened her mouth to say something, but he was sound asleep. He looked so young, much younger than she felt right at this moment. She kissed his cheek. She worried about her mother for another hour or so before she fell asleep.

The next morning came early and hard.

It wasn't quite dawn when Abee heard someone move onto the porch below them. One of the wood rocking chairs croaked under someone's weight. The person began to rock back and forth.

Abee opened her eyes to find the Bogle that had been tormenting her with the image of Everett's cousin, Elaine, looming over the bed. Abee gave the Bogle a soft smile. She grabbed a cotton robe from the closet and went down to see who was on the porch. Ma'am slept at the back of the house, so she never heard the front door or porch.

It was up to Abee to welcome or send away any intruders.

Hoping for the best, but terrified of the worst, Abee opened the heavy front door. She stepped out onto the porch to see who was there.

An ancient African-American was sitting in the rocking chair. Her skin was deep chocolate brown, and her hair was a shock of white up in a tight bun. She wore a long, old-fashioned black cotton dress with long sleeves. Abee peered through the dim light of pre-dawn. The woman was so old that Abee wasn't certain she was alive.

"The new Mrs. Beauchamp, I presume," the elderly woman said in crisp words.

"Abee Normal, ma'am," she said. "What can I . . . Well . . ."

Abee blinked. The elderly woman smiled and let Abee struggle with what to do next.

"How about I make us some tea?" Abee asked finally.

As if Abee had met with the ancient woman's approval, the elderly woman smiled.

"Would you like to come inside?" Abee asked.

"You don't want the neighbors to see me?" the elderly woman asked in the same crisp speech.

"I don't want the neighbors to see me!" Abee said with a grin.

"You don't have neighbors," the elderly woman said.

"We don't have neighbors," Abee said. She grinned at the elderly woman. "Ma'am was finishing her breakfast cookies when I went up to bed. The house is full of people. We need to get inside quickly if we want to have one."

"Those cookies *are* good," the elderly woman said.

Abee smiled. The elderly woman must know Ma'am.

"We expect some of the disagreeable relatives to show up and eat us out of house and home," Abee said. "We early birds need to get our own."

"How do you know that I'm not one of those disagreeable relatives?" the elderly woman sniffed.

"Instinct," Abee said.

The elderly woman gave her a broad grin, showing her gleaming dentures. Abee nodded.

"Watch yourself as you come in," Abee said. "The house has charms on it. If you feel uncomfortable, just let me know, and we'll head right back out."

"Don't worry, child," the elderly woman's voice shifted to kind. "I helped your Ma'am refresh them when you came to live in this house."

Instinctively, Abee went to the elderly woman's side to help her up. The elderly woman put her arm through Abee's elbow, and the girl helped the elderly woman shuffle the few steps down the porch and into the door. As they stepped through the doorway, the elderly woman stopped walking. The house seemed to sigh in greeting. The elderly woman smiled in response.

For all of the dark misuse of the exterior of the house, the inside of Ma'am's house was warm, light, and comfortable. The only signs of technology existed on Abee's third floor. The rest of the house was set up for conversation and comfort. The elderly woman took a deep breath, and she seemed to strengthen.

"Would you mind if I sit right there?" the elderly woman asked. She pointed to a soft rocking chair near the door. "I've walked a long way today."

"Not at all," Abee said. "You rest right there, and I'll get us some tea and cookies."

The elderly woman nodded her thanks. Abee went into the kitchen, where she filled the tea pot with cool well water from the sink faucet. Abee set the teapot on the stove. She looked around the kitchen.

"They aren't here," Abee said.

The elderly woman smiled.

"Try that cabinet on top of the refrigerator," the elderly woman said.

"Good thinking." Abee started back to the kitchen.

"Your Ma'am's been hiding good stuff up there since before I was a child," the elderly woman said. "You might just put some of that brandy that's up there in my tea."

"Yes, ma'am." Abee shot back to the elderly woman in the living room.

The tea was steeping in the pot when Ma'am came out from her first-floor rooms. She put her hand on Abee's shoulder and looked into her eyes.

"You ready for today?" Ma'am asked.

Abee shook her head. Ma'am put her hand on the side of Abee's face before leaving the kitchen to speak with their guest. Abee heard the women speak in hushed words. When Abee came out with a tray of tea, brandy, and breakfast cookies, the elderly woman was wiping her eyes. Ma'am took the tray from her.

"Abeegail Normal," Ma'am said. "This is Bertha Beauchamp."

"Nice to meet you, ma'am," Abee said. She held out her hand, and Bertha gave her a firm handshake. "Would you like some cream or sugar or . . ."

The elderly woman took the top off the teapot to smell the tea.

"This will be just fine," the elderly woman said with a smile. "You can go get dressed. Your Ma'am and I have been friends for longer than you've been alive."

"Bertha grew up in the Beauchamp household," Ma'am said. "She was Emery's grandfather's . . ."

Not wanting to offend, Ma'am's voice fell off.

"Mistress," Bertha said.

"Mother of his second family," Ma'am said.

"That, too," Bertha said. "You can guess that me and your Ma'am need a good catch-up."

Not sure how to respond, Abee gave Bertha a slight nod. Ma'am nodded to Abee, and the girl scooted up the stairs. On the third floor, Abee slipped into her own room. She grabbed a pair of jeans, some fitness shoes, and a top. Tall and thin, Abee didn't necessarily need a bra, so she skipped it rather than wake Emily or Jeremiah by rummaging through her drawers.

"Abee?" Emily asked.

Goji jumped off the bed to greet Abee. She greeted her dog before going to sit with Emily.

"I have to tell you something," Emily said.

"I'm listening," Abee said.

As she did when Emily was upset, Abee took Emily's hand. Abee assumed that Emily would want to talk about her relationship with Everett or possibly her hurt feelings that they kept it from her. But Emily had more important things on her mind.

"I wanted to tell you that . . . um . . ." Emily glanced over at Jeremiah.

The boy was awake and watching them closely.

"Tell her," Jeremiah said. "She won't be upset."

"What is it?" Abee asked, still thinking that Emily wanted to talk about Abee's relationship with Emily's twin.

"You know, my dad is dead," Emily said.

"I'm so sorry," Abee said, her voice full of sympathy for her sweet friend.

"I'm not," Emily said with anger in her voice. "He treated me like I was stupid."

Abee grinned at Emily's feisty nature. Emily grinned at Abee's grin. Emily sighed, and her eyes shot to Jeremiah.

"Just tell her," Jeremiah said.

"Well, I might be a little sad that Daddy is gone," Emily said. "And I'm kind of mad that he made me watch."

"He made you watch?" Abee asked. Rage coursed through her. She felt the sacred flame rising from her core.

"Oh look — your eyes turned blue," Emily said.

"It makes me very angry that your father made you watch him injure himself," Abee said.

"It's okay, Abee," Emily said. "He always needed someone to be his audience. I was just there."

Abee smiled at how generous Emily could be. Afraid that she might injure Emily with the sacred flame, Abee forced herself to calm down. Emily patted Abee's hand until Abee felt the sacred flame return to her core.

"There you are," Emily said with a grin.

"What did you want to tell me?" Abee asked.

"I want to go to college like you and Evie," Emily said. "Evie" was her and Abee's nickname for Everett. "I want to get a real job and live a real life. Not just a cared-for-like-a-doll life. I'm not a baby."

Abee gave Emily a soft smile.

"I'm not a doll," Emily said. "I want a job. I want a *real* life. I want to get married like you and Evie."

Emily nodded to Abee. Abee opened her mouth.

"Now don't you say I can't," Emily said. "I'm pretty smart. Maybe not as smart as you or Evie, but I'm smart enough. If I have help, I can do it."

"What would you like to do for a living?" Abee asked.

"I want to be a teacher, like Mr. Ted," Emily said. "Did you know that he's my uncle?"

"I learned that recently," Abee said.

"I think you treat me like a doll sometimes, too," Emily said, intentionally making an exaggerated pout. "Like a little baby."

"Probably," Abee said with a nod. "I love you and want you to be safe. The world is not always nice to people who are special, different."

"You're special," Emily said. "You're different."

"The world isn't always so nice to me," Abee said.

She gave Emily a soft grin. Emily nodded in agreement.

"Now that you're my sister, do you want my money, too?" Emily asked with such sincerity that Abee could only smile.

"No," Abee said. "I want something that's more valuable."

"What's that?" Emily asked.

"I want your love," Abee said.

Overwhelmed, Emily threw her arms around Abee. Emily's heft against Abee's near-skeletal frame caused them to swerve. Jeremiah laughed at them.

"I think it will be hardest for Evie," Abee said when she pulled back.

"Why?" Emily asked. "Does Evie think I'm an imbecile, too? Like Daddy did?"

Abee gasped. She saw Emily's sincerity and glanced at Jeremiah. The boy nodded to affirm that Emery had said that his daughter was an imbecile. Abee shook her head.

"You know Evie," Abee said. "He wants to be your champion, your knight in shining armor."

"I sure do!" Everett said from the doorway. "I wouldn't know what to do with myself otherwise."

"Emily wants to go to college," Abee said. "She wants to be a teacher like Mr. Ted."

"Sounds good to me," Everett said. He took two steps and dropped to his knees next to Abee's bed, where Emily was sitting. "You are not an imbecile."

Emily started to cry. Everett scooped up his twin, and Abee stepped back.

"I'll take Goji out to do her business," Abee said to anyone who was listening.

She kissed Emily's cheek and left the room. Abee dressed quickly in the bathroom. As they did every morning, she and Goji trotted down the stairs. Goji stopped at the first-floor landing to give an eardrum-bursting bark at Bertha in the living room.

"Go see," Abee said.

With her nose in the air, Goji made a slow trip to the visitor. The elderly woman put her hands down for Goji to smell. Goji took that as an invitation for the elderly woman to scratch her ears. Bertha laughed and cooed at the dog.

"Why don't you go for a run?" Ma'am asked.

"Seems kind of . . ." Abee shrugged.

"They are already lining up outside," Ma'am said.

Abee looked outside. Elaine, Everett and Emily's cousin, was sitting on the roof of her car. Abee gulped. The Bogle Abee had picked up in New Jersey had reflected to Abee her terror of this human Elaine. There were real reasons for Abee's terror. Elaine had ruthlessly bullied Abee when they were in elementary school. The human Elaine was a cruel child who had grown into an even crueler adult. There were also deeper and less-defined ways that Elaine was terrifying. Abee was doing her best to work through everything, but so much life was happening all at once. There wasn't much time for deep psychological thought.

"Go out the back," Ma'am said.

Abee started toward the back. She got to the back door, where she saw a brand-new horse barn. The barn must have been built while Abee was working as a paranormal investigator or studying or in New Jersey. Sam, the Mustang her friend Pen's father had bought for her, was standing in a new horse pen. Pen's horse and the stallion Everett preferred were also in the pen. Abee looked down to see that her riding boots were set next to the door. She put on her boots and grabbed her keys from the hook next to the door.

"Thanks, Ma'am," Abee called back to her Ma'am.

When she left the house, Goji headed out into the forest behind Ma'am's home. Abee was halfway to the new barn when Pen came out of it with a fork full of hay. She had checked that the horses had water and made sure that they had hay.

"Pen!" Abee said.

The two women hugged each other in greeting.

"Did you sleep well?" Pen asked.

"Not really," Abee said. "You?"

Pen shook her head.

"This is new," Abee said.

"My dad had it built," Pen said. "He said that it was a shame to have the horses at home when you might ride them if they were here."

"That's nice of him," Abee said.

"I thought we could go for a ride instead of a run today," Pen said.

"Sounds good to me," Abee said.

Everett, Abee, and Pen ran "together" (via cell phone) almost every day. Abee rubbed her hands together in anticipation of riding her beautiful Mustang.

"Listen . . ." Pen started.

"Don't go without me!" Everett called from Abee's window on the third floor.

Abee waved to Everett, and his head disappeared upstairs.

"I wanted to tell you," Pen said.

Abee turned her whole attention to Pen.

"I quit modeling," Pen said in a low tone.

"You did?" Abee asked.

Pen nodded.

"Is it a secret?" Abee asked.

"Just embarrassed," Pen said. "Evie used to go on and on about how I would hate modeling and I should go to college and blah, blah."

Abee remembered Everett's rants about Pen being too smart to "waste her life in modeling."

"What happened?" Abee asked.

"Oh," Pen sighed. "I'll tell you when he gets here. I feel better just telling you and seeing your reaction."

"What reaction?" Abee asked.

"Exactly," Pen said. "You just want me to be happy. I forget that. I just . . ."

Blushing, Pen nodded.

"It's true," Abee said. "It doesn't really matter what you do. I just want you to be happy."

Pen hugged Abee.

"Let's finish up so we can just ride," Pen said.

Behind the house, they could hear more than one car arrive. Car doors slammed, and the angry voices of arguing people wafted toward them. Pen and Abee focused on getting the horses ready for a ride. By the time Everett came out of the house, their horses were ready to go.

"Did Abee tell you?" Everett asked as he approached them.

"Tell me what?" Pen asked.

"Emily wants to go to college," Everett said.

Abee nodded.

"Sounds great to me," Pen said.

"She says that our father kept her from even wanting something else for her life," Everett said. "He told her that she was an imbecile."

"Uh," Pen said in a quick, disgusted exhale.

"That man . . ." Abee shook her head.

"He really has a poor opinion of women," Pen said. "He used to tell me that I should focus on 'marrying well.' Prick."

Realizing that she was speaking ill of the dead, Pen gasped and put her hand in front of her mouth.

"Sorry," Pen said.

Everett shrugged.

"Let's go look at the plantation," Abee said. "I can tell you what we've come up with so far."

"What you've what?" Everett's head jerked up to look at Abee.

"I didn't anticipate your father's death," Abee said. "And certainly, I would have never, ever guessed at the circumstances . . ."

She looked up from her horse, Sam, to see that she held Everett and Pen's attention.

"I've had months to think about what we could do about this Beauchamp financial situation," Abee said. "I think I've come up with a way to make it right."

"And?" Everett asked.

"We have a plan," Abee said. "I didn't know about this 'Founder's Document,' though. Did you give it to Jonas?"

Jonas Fremont was the head of the legal team that was managing Abee's inheritance, received only after her biological father had tried to murder her outright. He'd hung himself, too — a thought which caused Abee to scowl.

"Of course," Everett said, intimidated by Abee's dark look. "He's looking at it right now. I passed him on my way down the stairs."

"Everyone is an early riser," Abee said.

"Jonas and I are on New York time," Pen said.

"Me, too," Everett said. "But I slept in."

"You had to deal with all this family crap," Pen said. "That's bound to be exhausting. Not to mention the wedding-night sex."

Remembering that they'd just gone to sleep, Abee blushed. Everett shook his head at Pen's teasing.

"Let's get out of here before they find us," Everett said. "Anyone have water?"

"Ma'am gave me a thermos of coffee and those breakfast cookies," Pen said. "Some water, too."

They heard a heavy vehicle pull up to the house in front.

"Let's go," Everett said.

They mounted their horses. Intimidated by the noise and the gathering at the front of the house, they rode off in silence. Goji caught up with them by the time they entered the deep woods. They continued toward the Beauchamp Plantation. They passed the school where they'd gone to private elementary school and high school before they got to the Beauchamp plantation house. Bright yellow Police tape was strung from pillar to pillar along the front of the big, ostentatious front of the house.

No one seemed to be around.

"Did you go in yesterday?" Pen asked Everett.

Everett nodded. Abee and Pen watched him until he responded.

"I . . ." Everett shook his head. "I don't really know what to say. The rope that he . . . you know . . . . . . Anyway, it was still hanging there. The police detective said it was quite an engineering feat that he was able to get it up there and . . ."

Everett sighed.

"I don't know," Everett said. "The entry reeked of pee and shit — you know, from Dad — after he. . . uh . . . died."

Everett face reflected his anger and disgust.

"Emily said that he made her watch," Abee said. "I know that she exaggerates sometimes . . ."

"Like we all do," Pen said.

"Of course, he made her watch," Everett said. His brow dropped in a deep scowl. "He never did anything without an audience of adoring fans. God. Poor Em."

"Maybe you could ask her about it," Abee said.

"She's asleep now," Everett said with a nod. "But I will. I want to hear about your plan for this stupid plantation. My vote is gasoline and a match."

Abee smiled at him. She held out her hand, and he took it. Their eyes held for a moment. She saw his pain and anger in his eyes. She squeezed his hand.

"I want to hear about Pen," Abee said.

Relieved to talk about something else, Everett pounced on the idea.

"You've been avoiding us for long enough!" Everett said.

"She's not modeling anymore," Abee said.

"What?" Everett asked.

"I . . ." Pen blushed.

"Let's go around back," Abee said. "We can get to the tunnel and see what's going on there."

They rode for a few minutes to the entrance to the tunnel under the Beauchamp mansion.

"How do we get in?" Pen asked, shaking the gate.

"I still have the key," Abee said.

She took the key from her pocket and held it up. She unlocked the padlock that held the gate. They pushed it open and went inside the tunnel to the comfortable sitting area.

"Doesn't look like they came down here," Everett said.

"Weird, huh?" Abee asked. "There are water bottles over there."

Pen looked around the room. Pen scowled. Abee grabbed a water bottle from the stack against the wall. Using a bottle of water, she poured water for Goji.

"It gives some credence to the idea that Abee's mom wasn't well," Pen said.

Abee nodded. She and Pen flopped onto the couch while Everett took a chair. Pen took Ma'am's breakfast cookies from her bag and passed out the travel mugs of coffee. Tucked away from the chaos, they were very simple eighteen-year-old best friends hanging out. They began to relax. Having finished drinking her water, Goji jumped on the couch to sit between Abee and Pen.

"So . . ." Abee said, turning to Pen.

"There isn't much to tell," Pen said.

"Tell us what there is to tell," Everett said.

"I went to this party with . . ." Pen named a famous model who'd been Pen's lover for the last six months. "I was standing with the models, you know, all squished together like we do. Some pro football players were there. Basketball players. I went to go to the bathroom and ran into this guy from MIT."

Pen nodded.

"Like ran into him," Pen said. "Boom."

Abee and Everett laughed.

"His drink went all over me," Pen said. "I . . . Anyway, he felt awful. He was sure that he had caused the whole thing. We started talking, and it was like talking to you all. It felt really nice to talk to someone with a brain. Before I knew it, we were talking about something — I don't remember what. Psychics on Mars, I think."

Pen nodded. Used to Pen's conversation style, Abee and Everett waited for her to collect her thoughts.

"I mean, it's not like he's *my* type," Pen said with a shake of her head. "And anyway, he has a girlfriend. We were there, geeking out about the new findings on Mars, and my *date* came up."

Pen said the word "date" as if she were saying something disgusting.

"She starts freaking out," Pen said. "Full-on breakdown — jealous, betrayed, like I had *done* something to her by talking to this guy. Somehow, I got her into a taxi and back to my place," Pen said. "She just escalated. I tried to defuse her, but I don't have any experience with hysterical people. I mean, it's all good and well in theory, but when you're standing there? It's a whole different thing."

"My heart was beating so fast I thought I was having a heart attack and she was . . ."

Pen pulled her hair back to show a recently healed pink scar behind her ear.

"She hit me with a vase," Pen said. "Nearly took my ear off. She probably would have killed me if I hadn't locked myself on the balcony. She proceeded to break everything in my apartment. Everything."

Abee reached out to touch Pen's scar. She glanced at Everett. She could tell by the look on Everett's face that he felt as awful as Abee did that Pen had gone through this without them. Goji put her head on Pen's lap. Pen rubbed Goji's big, floppy ears.

"My neighbor, who also happens to be male, saw me on the balcony," Pen said. "We share the balcony, so it was really his balcony, too. He dragged me into his apartment and called the cops. He told me in the hospital that his dad used to beat up his mom until she left. They lived in domestic-violence shelters for a while."

"He took me to the hospital and stayed with me the whole time," Pen said.

"What happened to . . .?" Abee asked about the famous model.

"The cops came," Pen said. "They were going to arrest her, but she talked them out of it. She said that I had done most of the damage. Since I wasn't there, they took her word. I mean, she's really beautiful and famous. You can't really blame them. You can imagine what my *dad* had to say to their Sergeant about that."

"Your parents found out?" Abee asked. "Where was I?"

"You were almost killed by your bio dad and dealing with your transformation and everything else," Pen said. "We run together, yah, but just over the phone so you don't see me."

"I was just across the river!" Everett said.

"I just couldn't, Evie," Pen said. "I was just . . . mortified and . . ."

Pen fell silent for what felt like a long time.

"Mostly, I was so embarrassed," Pen said. "This is the kind of thing that happens to *other* people, not me."

"Oh, Pen," Abee said.

She leaned forward and hugged Pen. Everett got up to hug her when Abee released Pen. He sat on the arm of the couch next to Pen rather than return to his chair.

"Mom hired a crew to clean and fix my apartment while I was in the hospital," Pen said. "Dad dealt with the police, but when I was finally home? My machine was full of cancellations. Even my agent dumped me. My *girlfriend* told everyone some story about me being a crazy drug addict. When I finally got a chance to talk to my agent, she wasn't even surprised that it was, you know . . . the girlfriend's fault. My agent said that she'd done it a few times before. A few times! I'm the first time the police were called. Otherwise, people just let it go because . . . My agent didn't take me back, of course. She can't go against her because she's so hot right now."

"Oh, Pen, how awful," Abee said.

"Yeah," Pen said with a nod. "I was going to give up — you know, come home — when the guy from the party called me. I don't know how he got my number, but he did. He called to say that MIT was having an orientation. He wondered if I might want to go."

Abee held her breath when Pen nodded.

"My parents came with me," Pen said. She lifted her shoulders in a big shrug. "I was pretty black and blue — I mean, my mom put some makeup on me to cover it. No one really cared. We saw the school and went to the Physics Department. The guy at the party, he'd mentioned me to his physics professor. They showed me around the Psychics building.

"My dad was all — 'My daughter was accepted her last fall. She has the grades from this term to transfer here. What will it take for her to start in the fall?'" Pen said. "You know how he is."

"So do you go to MIT now?" Everett asked.

"Next fall," Pen said with a nod. "I finished my term at NYU and moved to Boston, though. I hate to say it, but I was kind of afraid of being in New York after all of that. I mean, I changed the locks, and Mom had everything all cleaned up, but . . . That woman who was my girlfriend came by a few times. Tried to get in."

Pen took a deep breath and shivered.

"I could still see the gouges in the wood floors," Pen said. "And stuff. I mean, I was going to stay at school, but then she called me. I mean, she called and left about a thousand messages, but she tricked me into answering."

"The nerve of that woman!" Abee said.

"Bitch," Everett said.

"Yeah," Pen said. "She said that she didn't remember anything that happened because she was high. I guess they got high on cocaine and opium in the bathroom while I was talking to the MIT guy."

"She's certainly responsible for getting high!" Everett said.

"I know, right?" Pen shook her head. "Of course, she said it was my fault for talking to the MIT guy. And you know what?"

Pen nodded.

"She was right," Pen said. "She saw how much more comfortable I was with the guy. I was more comfortable, more genuine with that guy. She mistook it as romance. Really, it was just being around someone with a brain."

"That doesn't excuse what she did!" Abee said.

"It was her totally fault!" Everett said. "Pen!"

"Oh, no, it was her fault," Pen said. "She really brained me, too. I still have a concussion."

"Why didn't you tell us?" Abee asked.

"Like I said, you guys have had your own life-and-death dramas going on," Pen said.

"Still," Everett said.

"I was going to tell you this weekend when you came to Boston to look at your dad's houses," Pen said. "I mean, I'm living in Boston, so I would be like '*Ta Da!*'"

"Are you working?" Abee asked.

Even though Pen's parents were wealthy, Pen had always liked to make her own money. She didn't like the strings her parents put on her spending.

"Not right now," Pen said. "I'm suffering in dependency."

Pen lifted a shoulder slightly in a shrug.

"I go to therapy mostly," Pen said. "Sit in coffee shops. Mope around. Stuff like that. And . . ."

Pen took a breath.

"It's really helped — you know, therapy, space," Pen said. "Mom and Dad come to see me almost every weekend. Jeremiah calls every day. I've worked through a lot of stuff. Including all of this crap."

"That's a good outcome, but . . . ," Abee said. "Really."

Everett shook his head. Pen nodded.

"I know," Pen said. She looked at Everett and winced. "Do you know that we're cousins?"

Everett nodded.

"Your mom is Emery's sister," Everett said. "I was kind of blown away about Ted though."

"Yeah," Pen said. "I didn't find out until this year. So I didn't know, either."

Pen nodded, and Everett smiled. Pen turned to Abee and grinned.

"Welcome to the family," Pen said.

Abee laughed. Pen grinned.

"Speaking of family . . ." Abee said. "Any ideas about what you want to do with this place?"

"I have — gasoline and a match," Everett said, bitterly.

"Tear it down and sell the land," Pen said. "It's caused so much pain for generations. It shouldn't stand. My mom told me all about growing up here. Her dad was super abusive, and you know what an asshole Emery became."

Pen shook her head.

"We should destroy the whole thing," Pen said.

"What if we remake it?" Abee asked.

"I have no idea what that means," Pen said. She looked at Everett, and he shook his head. "Enlighten us, Mrs. Beauchamp."

"Ms. Normal-Beauchamp," Abee said.

Realizing that she hadn't talked to Everett about names, she wrinkled her nose and looked at Everett.

"I'd be happy being 'Mr. Normal,'" Everett said with a chuckle.

They grinned. For a few minutes, they drank their coffee and ate their breakfast cookies. Pen cleared her throat.

"So . . ." Pen said. "What's the plan?"

Abee grinned at her impatient friend. Pen was like a dog with a bone. She never let anything go.

"Well, I don't know until they look at this Founder's Document but . . ." Abee said.

"Tell us what you know!" Pen said.

Abee looked at Everett and he nodded.

"Okay," Abee said. "Well . . ."

Abee sighed. She took a breath to start talking but then let it out. Her Bogle appeared in front of her. Abee took in the Bogle's disgust and cruel face. She blinked. Her heart still raced with terror, but she nodded.

She could be afraid and tell her friends her plan anyway. She swallowed hard.

"So . . ." The word came out in a kind of squeak. She cleared her throat. "The first thing you have to remember is . . ."

Abee nodded.

"You know, a corporation has been determined to have the rights of a person," Abee said.

Everett gasped.

"That's brilliant," Everett said.

"Case law since the Supreme Court decision has pressed the law so that a corporation *is* technically a person," Abee said.

"What?" Pen asked. "What does that mean?"

"We're going to create a corporation out of the Beauchamp Plantation," Abee said. "Our shares will be privately held. We've come up with three ways to get shares.

The first is the most obvious. There's a bunch of debt on the plantation, so we need money. People can buy in."

"But only family?" Everett asked.

"Only members of the Beauchamp family," Abee said. "The number people who want to buy in will determine the share cost. We need to pay off the debt and create a fund for expenses. But here's the novel part."

She looked at Everett and smiled. She looked at Pen.

"The second group is people who were enslaved on this plantation," Abee said. "The problem with that is that the records aren't great. We've been waiting to get down here because I remembered that stack of stuff. I think it's plantation records."

Abee pointed to a stack of old ledger books.

"You can buy into the plantation or work into the plantation," Abee said. "And . . .there's a third group. These are people who have Beauchamp genes. They're likely to fit into one or the other category. We will take those as they come."

"How many people do you think will be a part of it?" Pen asked.

"Lots. Your father has already talked to me about buying shares for himself, your mother, you and Jeremiah. Turns out he has Beauchamp genes, as well," Abee said. "Oh, also, if you sell shares, you can sell them only into the pool. You can't sell to someone who doesn't fit into one of these groups."

"What about the folks the plantation was given to?" Everett asked. "After the Union Soldiers came through, they imprisoned my great-great-grandfather, you know, because he was a traitor. They gave the plantation to the freed slaves."

Everett nodded.

"They were slaves from all of the plantations around," Everett said. "They worked the land until the plantation was jerked out of their hands when my lying, cheating great-grandfather arranged some amnesty deal with Washington. There's a family in town that used to scream at my dad about it."

"A fourth group," Abee said. "As we go, we'll probably find a lot more people who deserve shares."

No one said anything for a moment while they digested Abee's information.

"You think this will work?" Pen asked.

"Who knows?" Abee asked. "Worst case, Everett is the eldest son of Emery. He'll inherit everything. I'll pay off the debt, and things will stay the same."

Pen looked at Everett, and he shrugged.

"You have enough money?" Pen asked.

"I have enough money to buy this place and your house and . . . shit, most of the county," Abee said with a grin. "That is, if I was in a spending mood."

"Why haven't you . . .?" Pen asked and then stopped talking.

"Why haven't I?" Abee asked.

"Taken a trip, bought some clothing, got your hair done, your nails, shit — bought shoes," Pen said.

"Because my friend Pen was in Boston on the sly," Abee said, with a smile. "And, I don't know — I'm kind of embarrassed. This a fortune that was created in human suffering. It feels . . . bad."

Abee nodded. Rather than respond, she got up and walked to the stack of books in the back. She turned over the cover of the one on the top. Sighing, she turned around.

"We should head back," Abee said. She looked at her Bogle and nodded. "Face the music."

Pen nodded. Everett went to Pen to hug her. They were just starting to walk out of the underground room when the horrifying figure of Elaine appeared.

Real as life, Elaine the Terrible was walking toward them. The look on her face could seer steak. Goji growled and came to Abee's side.

Abee stopped short. She blinked.

"What the hell are you doing?" Elaine asked.

Finally ready to deal with Elaine, Abee stepped forward. Everett intervened.

"This is private property," Everett said. "Get the hell out of here."

"*My* private property," Elaine said.

"How is it your property?" Everett asked.

"I paid Emery for it," Elaine aid.

"If you were dumb enough to give my father money, that's your problem," Everett said. "You are not now, nor will you ever be the eldest Beauchamp male. Your loser father won't be the eldest Beauchamp male, either. Only the eldest male can own this land."

Elaine gaped at Everett. She looked at Abee and sneered.

"You should leave," Abee said.

"Go on." Pen's voice caused Elaine's head to jerk to look at Pen. "Just in case you don't know who I am, I'm Gina's daughter. Get the hell out of *my* family home."

"You can't be here, either," Elaine said weakly. She turned to Abee. "Her kind's never been welcomed in this house."

"I own this house and the plantation now," Everett said. "My *wife* is welcome wherever I am."

"You *married* that monkey?" Elaine asked.

"Get out," Pen said.

"Fine," Elaine said. "I'll see you in court. I will get my due."

Before she left, she spit at Abee.

"I'd watch yourself," Abee said. "I could just lose my grip on the dog's collar."

Elaine looked down at Goji. Solid muscle with black fur, Goji's hackles were up. She gave a deep growl and looked leaned against the restraint of her collar. Elaine spun in place and trotted down the tunnel and out the door.

When she was gone, Pen cheered. Everett kissed Abee's lips. But Abee shook her head.

"It's going to be hard," Abee said. "There are a lot of forces that don't want change. They don't want something new. We'd be smarter just to light a fire. Poof."

Abee gestured with her hands as if the fire consumed the room they were in.

"We'll just have to change their minds," Everett said.

Abee glanced at Everett and then at Pen.

"What else are we going to do with our lives?" Pen asked.

"If we don't clean this shit up, who will?" Everett asked.

Abee nodded because she knew they expected her to. They made their way out of the tunnel to their horses.

Once they were on their horses, Pen and Everett fell into an easy conversation about school. Abee rode behind them.

She wasn't ready to lead this battle.

But she would lead it none-the-less.

Abee looked at her Bogle and smiled.

"Thank you," Abee said to her Bogle. "I release you."

The face of Elaine melted away. She was looking into the actual face of the Bogle. Although its face was not human, Abee could make out a mouth and two eyes. She thought she saw a small nose or more like nostrils. The creature was obsidian in color, so black that it was nearly reflective. Its body looked soft and hard at the same time, yet flexible, while still holding its form. She'd never seen anything like it.

Abee felt as if the creature was trying to tell her something.

Abee reached out her hand to the Bogle. The Bogle put up something that looked like a hand. Palm to palm, their hands touched.

"Be careful," the Bogle said in as clear a language as if it had spoken. "Your freedom insights their rage."

"Whose?" Abee asked.

"Now, you are asking the correct question." The Bogle nodded. "Why did you not go to school? Why did you go to the Emerald Mound? Why did the Mother of the

Sacred Flame wish to help a little human like you? Why were you and I thrown together?"

"You think Ma'am . . ." Abee said.

"No." The Bogle was firm. "Not Ma'am. Not your little friends. Your little mind."

The Bogle's other hand touched Abee's forehead.

"Listen." She heard the Bogle loud and clear. "Listen. Every single day. You will begin to hear."

Abee nodded.

"You will promise? To hear?" The Bogle leaned forward as if to listen to Abee's response.

"I promise," Abee whispered. She wasn't exactly sure what she was promising, only that this creature needed her to promise.

"Everything depends on you." The Bogle nodded again. "Every single thing."

"What does that mean?" Abee asked.

"Listen," The Bogle repeated. "If you cannot, we are all lost."

Seeing that she wouldn't get any more information from the Bogle, she nodded.

"Thank you," Abee said. She flushed with genuine emotion. "I never could have done this without you. Thank you."

"You are ready." The Bogle backed its hand away.

"I am ready," Abee whispered.

The Bogle nodded.

"Would you like to go home?" Abee asked.

The Bogle looked surprised. The Bogle nodded. Abee clapped her hands and flicked her fingers.

"Take the sacred flame home," Abee said.

She pointed to a thin line of blue flame that floated in the air. The Bogle gave Abee a deep bow. The sacred flame surrounded the Bogle. With one last look at Abee, the Bogle disappeared.

"Abee?" Everett called from up ahead.

"She was just behind us," Pen said.

Abee took one last look to where the Bogle had been and pressed her thighs into the Mustang's side. They sped up to where her friends were waiting.

"There you are!" Everett said, looking relieved.

"Sorry. I guess I'm a little intimidated," Abee said.

"Don't be," Pen said.

"We'll do this together," Everett said.

Abee looked from Pen to Everett. Their confidence in her was palpable. She smiled.

"Let's get it started," Abee said.

Together, they rode the rest of the way home to Ma'am's house.

EIGHT

The case of:
Crazy as . . .

"Emily is almost ready to move into her room," Abee said.

She was brushing her mother's long dark hair. Even though Abee's skin was a deep black color, her mother's skin was white. Joanna's hair was fine in texture, but curly. Since Joanna's return from the hospital, Abee had spent every morning taking care of her mother's hair. First, she brushed it. Then Abee braided the long hair so it wouldn't get tangled. She passed the time by updating her on what was going on around her.

Joanna's eyes were open, but she had yet to say anything. It was weird. Abee hoped that these little, mundane details of her life would help bring her mother back to herself.

Ma'am set down a vile-smelling cup of tea on the bedside table. Abee nodded to Ma'am. The tea would help strengthen Joanna in her battle against the Multiple Sclerosis that had destroyed her nerves and would help heal her mother's broken heart.

"I was really surprised," Abee said, stroking her mother's hair with the brush. "I thought that Emily would

like everything painted pink, you know, like she had it at . . .
uh . . . her childhood home."

Abee felt a flash of self-rage. She shouldn't have
mentioned the Beauchamps mansion. Joanna had nearly
died there. Abee bit back her self-rage to continue her light
conversation. For most of Abee's life, Joanna had done all of
the talking. Now that it was Abee's turn, she'd promised
herself that she would not mess it up.

"She said that pink was a baby's color," Abee said
with a forced chuckle. "I'm sure that this is a gripping
controversy for you. You're probably thinking: 'Come on,
Abee. What did you paint her walls?' A light yellow, not
quite butter, but darker than cream. Actually, it's really
beautiful. Jeremiah helped paint the white trim. It's clean
and nice. Emily's on the second floor in the guest room
across from you.

"Ma'am says that Uncle Al was in that room when
you were growing up," Abee said. "Jeff, Gina, and Jane were
up where I am. Emily didn't want to stay up there with me.
She said it was too far to go."

Abee shrugged.

"I don't mind the climb," Abee said. "Plus, I get a
whole floor to myself."

Abee reached over to get the hair band from the
table. She put the hair band on her wrist. Picking up the tea,
she gave it to her mother.

"Why don't you drink a bit before we finish up?" Abee asked. "Ma'am has sweetened it with that wonderful wild honey from the bees we caught in the forest."

Joanna's blue eyes looked at Abee as the girl set the mug of tea into her mother's hands. Joanna looked at the tea.

"You like this tea," Abee said. "It helps."

Joanna trusted Abee implicitly. She took a long drink of the tea.

"Good," Abee said. "When you're done, I'll read your tea leaves — give you a prediction for your day."

As if she were trying to understand what Abee had said, Joanna's eyebrows went up and down for a few minutes. Abee took that as a good sign. When Joanna had first come home, she wasn't able to move anything visible. The eyebrow movement was new. Her face was as still and placid as a statue.

Abee touched the tea cup, and Joanna drank it until it was empty. Thank God, Joanna was still able to swallow and digest. Abee took the cup from Joanna. She looked into the tea leaves and listened to the deepest part of her intuition as well as to her aching heart.

"It says that you are healing," Abee said with a big smile. "I know — it said that yesterday and the day before. But . . ."

Abee shrugged.

"That's either what's happening, or I suck at reading tea leaves," Abee said, with a laugh. She kissed her mother's face. "Good job drinking the tea. Thank you."

Abee was silent for a few minutes while she settled into braiding her mother's hair.

"Where was I . . .?" Abee asked out loud. She tried to keep a list of innocuous things to speak to her mother about every morning. Emily usually made the list. "Emily's room. That's right. I thought she'd want a four-poster bed, but she told me that she hates those."

Abee chuckled.

"Who knew?" Abee said. "She wanted the bed that was in there. You know, the one with the wood frame and headboard. We redid the floors and Uncle Al gave us a lovely light-green rug. We ordered light-green sheets, and Ma'am made some Roman shades in the same color. It's really coming together."

Abee nodded.

"Well, she seems really happy," Abee said. "Ma'am took Emily to enroll in community college. She's going to start next term, which is pretty exciting. Of course, you remember that Pen's at MIT, right?"

Joanna's eyes looked vague, so Abee pressed on.

"She's settling in, as well," Abee said. "Jeff — you know, Pen's dad —helped her move into the dorm. She has to stay in the dorm for the first year or so. After what happened, you know, with Pen's girlfriend, she was pretty nervous about living in the dorm. But she seems to like her roommate. That's good. She and Evie meet at least once on the weekend to talk and connect. We still talk every day."

Abee moved to set the brush down. As she moved, the diamond-encrusted wedding band on her left ring finger flashed in the light. With surprising strength, Joanna grabbed Abee's hand. Joanna's eyebrows furrowed. Her mouth pinched as if she wanted to say something.

Knowing that it was best for Joanna, Abee waited while her mother tried to speak. But the moment passed. Joanna's face went placid again. Her hand dropped Abee's left hand.

"You remember that Evie went back to Princeton," Abee said quickly, to cover over her sorrow. "He left right after you were hurt. I guess you were in still in a coma then."

Every time Joanna did something like that, Abee's heart rose with hope that her mother would return to her. But those moments passed almost as quickly as they came.

"We talked about him staying here but finally agreed that he kind of had to go to school," Abee said. "He's got to do well there so he can take care of Emily. I've got to do well at school, too, so that I can help take care of Emily and . . ."

Abee sighed rather than say the word "everything."

Abee looked at her mother. She hoped that her mother never knew about Abee's plan to leave her mother and this place forever. If Abee had gone to Princeton with her beloved Everett, she would not be here now to help her mother. Abee fell silent.

There was nothing more important to Abee than helping her mother. She understood this now in a visceral way that she couldn't have imagined when she'd made the plan to escape. Abee put the band into the end of her mother's long braid of hair, where it would stay until Abee or Ma'am bathed Joanna this evening.

"I thought you might want to listen to your meditation music this morning," Abee said.

She turned on the mp3 player and put the headset over the top of her mother's head. The music was tones and sounds that were designed to help Joanna's brain heal. Hair brushing and vile tea over, the music relaxed Joanna. She would sleep until midday, which gave Abee all morning to work on her schoolwork.

Abee kissed her mother's head.

"I love you, Mom," Abee said.

She squeezed her mother's shoulders and left the room. She found Emily waiting for her on the second-floor landing.

"How is she?" Emily asked.

Emily's voice had a classic slur and lisp associated with her Down syndrome.

"The same," Abee said.

"Sorry, Abee," Emily said. "You must be sad."

Abee gave a slight nod.

"What are you up to today?" Abee asked.

"Today, I am going with Reginald to my father's house," Emily said.

Ever since Emily and Everett's father, Emery, had hanged himself in front of Emily, Emily called the Beauchamps Mansion "her father's house." She hadn't been back there since. Reginald had been the family butler. His wife, Alice, had been the family housekeeper. For most of Emily and Everett's lives, he and his wife had run the Beauchamps Mansion. They had been fired by Emery only weeks before he'd hanged himself.

Abee had hired them to help through the transition. Heirs to the Beauchamp family, Reginald and Alice were happy to participate in Abee's plan to convert ownership of the estate to all of the heirs.

"I am going to get the clothes that I want," Emily said. "My computer and books and stuff. So I'll be ready for school."

Emily nodded.

"It's probably going to take you all week," Abee said.

"I know," Emily said. "I'm just excited to get settled into my room."

Abee grinned at Emily. The girl had been through so much in the last month or so. Yet, as always, her heart was pure gold.

"Did you get breakfast?" Abee asked.

"You ask me that at every meal," Emily said. "I'm eighteen years old. I can figure out when to eat."

Abee smiled at Emily's gentle reproach.

"I'm not a baby, Abee," Emily said.

"Oh, Em," Abee said. She hugged the girl. "You will always be my little Emily."

"I guess that's okay," Emily said, hugging her back. "That's how sisters are."

Abee smiled. Emily was still thrilled that Abee had married her twin, Everett, making them sisters *for life*. Abee smiled. There was a knock on the front door, and they stopped to listen.

Reginald had arrived. Ma'am called Emily down. Abee gave the girl one last smile before heading up the flight of stairs to her room.

Finally alone, Abee went through her list.

She'd tried to call Everett this morning. Check.

Her mother was cared for and asleep. Check.

Emily was on her way to an eventful day. Check.

Ma'am was busy with plans for the new corporation. Check.

Her household chores were completed. Check.

Her dog, Goji, had been out for a long romp in the forest. She was now sleeping on Abee's bed. Check.

Only after everything was taken care of did Abee allow herself the indulgence of crying. For a few quiet moments, Abee gave into her sorrow.

Her computer video phone rang. Abee looked up. Everett's image flashed on her screen. Her hands slashed at her tears before she reached over to the computer.

"There you are!" Abee said.

No one was there. She could hear talking, but he wasn't there.

"Evie?" Abee asked.

The screen was dark, as if it were covered in cloth. There was a bright light behind it.

Abee looked at the clock on her wall.

Everett was in class.

His phone had dialed itself.

She sighed. She and Everett kept missing each other.

Before her mother's injuries and his father's death, Abee, Everett, and Pen had run together via Bluetooth headsets and their telephones every morning. Now Abee took care of her mother during that time. She had class or Emily or household chores or studying for her own schoolwork or corporation work or a thousand other things that took up the rest of her day.

When Everett tried to reach her, she was busy.

When she tried to reach Everett, he was busy.

The whole thing was . . .

Abee shook the thoughts from her head. No need to go crazy today.

She opened her laptop. She was working on a project for her American History class at Hampton University. This section was called "Personal History." Students were to look into their own personal history for aspects of American history that were left out of history books. They'd spent a week working on how their ancestors got to this country. They'd spent the next week interviewing their parents and grandparents about their personal experience of Jim Crow, the redlining, Black Panthers, and interactions with the heroes of the African-American Experience.

This week was simply called "Family Shame." They were encouraged to look into their family closets. About half of the class was looking into some kind of sexual violence in their family history. About a fourth of the class had someone in their family who had "passed for white." There were a few people looking into their familial connection to plantation life.

At first, Abee wasn't sure what to look into. She couldn't very well talk about her Ma'am's experience of being captured and enslaved. She couldn't tell them about Ma'am's journey to America on one of the last slave ships, in 1859. Certainly, her mother's situation with Emery was too raw for Abee to even think about. Her biological father's family history seemed as inconsequential to her as he had been, except, of course, when he was trying to kill her.

Abee decided to research mental illness.

Her grandmother, Joanna's mother, was locked away in a mental hospital. When Abee had inherited some serious money from her biological father, she, her Uncle Al, and Ma'am had been able to move her grandmother to a nicer facility. The new facility was cleaner, and the staff seemed kinder, but Abee's grandmother was still under lock and key.

According to Ma'am, throughout history, African-American women had spent a lot of time in mental hospitals.

Abee's teacher had been fascinated with the topic when Abee had brought it up.

"There is very little academic work done about African-Americans and mental health," he'd said. "Certainly, there's nothing I know of about mental-health incarceration as it relates to these larger issues we talk about."

He'd asked if anyone else had someone mentally ill in their family. Almost everyone had "pinged" to say "Yes." But when he asked if anyone wanted to join Abee in researching this part of the African-American experience, no one had wanted to join her project.

As in so many other things now, Abee was on her own.

She had learned some fascinating things. African-Americans had a 200% higher risk of being diagnosed with a serious mental illness, such as the schizophrenia Abee's grandmother had. Some researchers suggest that this is because sexual assault, violence, and homelessness were more common in African-Americans. Other research suggested that African-Americans were simply over-diagnosed with severe mental illness.

"We get hysterical when we're surrounded by bullshit," Abee said to herself.

Her friend, Tippi the Sprite, appeared on her desk. Abee nodded hello, and the five-inch high fairy fluttered her wings, sending spark-like glitter all over the room. Abee and Ma'am had freed Tippi from a Hobgoblin that had held her and her princess captive. Since her rescue, Tippi spent most of her time with Abee.

Tippi's light always made Abee feel a little brighter. She smiled at Tippi, and the tiny fairy showered her in glittery light.

Abee's email pinged. Hoping it was Everett, she clicked over to look.

Her request for her grandmother's records had finally been approved. Her grandmother's personal caseworker at the swanky mental-health hospital had sent Abee everything she'd been able to find. The email said that Ma'am had given the caseworker another name for Abee's grandmother. The caseworker had been able to obtain records dating back to when her grandmother was sixteen years old. The email ended with a caution.

"Be very careful with yourself, Abee. This stuff is pretty brutal."

Abee snorted. It felt like everything in her life carried an air of the "brutal" right now. Abee clicked the link, and the files began to download to her computer. She got up to turn on her electric kettle.

With everything that was going on, Abee kept forgetting to eat. Ma'am had put a small refrigerator and a microwave in Abee's room. Abee took out a carton of cream. Ma'am had stocked the refrigerator while Abee was in with Joanna. There was a plastic container that said "Breakfast." There was one for "Lunch" and "Dinner," too. Abee grabbed her protein smoothie from the tiny freezer and put it in the microwave for 30 seconds. The electric kettle clicked off.

Abee liked her strong tea, so she stuck three Earl Grey teabags into the cup. She'd just finished when the microwave dinged. Abee shook her smoothie and turned back to her computer.

The files were still downloading.

Abee drank down her smoothie. She went to her bathroom to wash out the bottle. Like everyone the world over, once in the bathroom, she had to go. She washed her hands and went back into her room. The room smelled of bergamot from the tea.

The files were still downloading.

"Damn," Abee said.

Tippi nodded. Abee took out her teabags, added some cream, and set the teabags in the bag for compost. She took her tea back to her computer.

The files had finally finished downloading. Abee clicked to extract the files and leaned back. She'd almost finished her tea when the files had finally finished extracting.

She clicked on the file that said "Kuhn Memorial Hospital 1961." Doing mental math, Abee realized that her grandmother would have been 16 years old in 1961. While the file opened, Abee typed the name of the hospital into her search engine and clicked on the link. Tippi flew to the top of Abee's computer screen so she could read along with Abee.

Kuhn Memorial Hospital was a public hospital in Vicksburg, MS, about an hour's drive from where she sat. The most recent videos were from ghost hunters. Abee yawned.

"Everything's haunted," Abee mumbled.

She continued reading the website. Hospital closed in 1989. Opened in 1832 in response to a smallpox epidemic in Vicksburg. It was run by George R. Burchett and then by his son and then by grandson and then by his great-grandson.

"Well, that's weird," Abee said. Tippi nodded.

Civil War wounded were treated at the hospital until Vicksburg surrendered to the Union Army on July 4, 1863. According to the website she was reading, the Union army laid siege to Vicksburg for 47 days. The fall of Vicksburg and Lee's loss at Gettysburg are considered to be the turning point of the Civil War.

Abee looked into her tea cup. Empty. She got up to turn on the pot again.

"Sounds like there's good reason for a haunting there," Abee said. "You've got smallpox epidemic, Civil War wounded, a siege . . ."

Tippi pointed to where the website talked about Yellow Fever killing doctors and nurses.

"Exactly," Abee said. "There was also a locked mental ward and a prison ward in that hospital. Probably where my grandmother was kept."

Tippi nodded.

"Okay," Abee said. "That's probably enough to look at the file."

Abee clicked to open the Kuhn Memorial file. The file that opened was for: Alicia Harris. Abee shook her head. Her grandmother's name was "Neviah." They called her "Nev."

"Alicia Harris = Neviah Erie Normal." Someone had scrawled across the top of the first page.

"I was just about to ask," Abee said with a chuckle.

It was only then that Abee remembered Ma'am telling her that her grandmother had made up all of the "Normal" names.

Abee clicked open the file. She read quickly. The medical file included several newspaper clippings. Abee looked up a few names and then read the medical file again. Trying to put everything together, Abee leaned back in her chair.

Alicia Harris had protested racism at an anti-segregation rally to protest Mississippi's then-Governor Ross Barnett. That fact was clear. Alicia and two of her girlfriends had left the protest together. That's where the facts got thin.

Alicia was taken to the emergency room by her father and mother three hours after the rally had ended. Alicia told the doctors that she'd been raped by four or five, maybe as many as seven, white boys from the white high school in town. The nurse who did the intake wrote that the white boys had told Alicia that they would kill her if she told anyone.

The doctor wrote: "Hallucinating."

Alicia's two friends had gone to the hospital with Alicia and her father but left before being treated. There is a note that Alicia told the nurse that her friends left after hearing the doctor call her and her friends "Negro whores."

Alicia's parents refused to budge. It was 1961, not 1861. This was a state hospital. They wanted their daughter to be treated for her trauma.

The doctor recommended in-patient treatment. Alicia's parents left their daughter with the doctor.

After being raped, Alicia went to the Emergency Room when she was 16 years old. She didn't get leave the mental hospital until she was 21 years old. Nine months after her incarceration, Alicia had given birth to a child. There was no record of what happened to the child.

There were plenty of records for what was done to Alicia.

Through it all, Alicia never wavered. She remained adamant that she was raped by those white boys. In response, she had every form of "modern" psychiatric treatment known at that time — ice baths, long-form electric shock treatments, drugs of all shapes and sizes, and other horrors.

In this protective care, Alicia happened to give birth again in 1965. There is no notation about who the father might have been or how this miraculous conception event came about. There was only a note that a child was born. That's all.

Abee shook her head. She started pacing the floor of her room.

"Fuck!" Abee yelled and kicked her chair.

Everything came together — Abee's rage at her mother's situation, her frustration over not being able to connect with her friends, her anger with herself for not being able to handle it all, and now the brutal unfairness of her grandmother's situation. Each situation folded into the next. Soon, blue smoke was coming off Abee's shoulders. Abee caught a glimpse of herself in the mirror.

She was surrounded by blue flame. Her clothing wasn't on fire, nor did she feel hot. The smoke was some kind of vapor or moisture in the air which today smelled like jasmine. Wincing, she decided to eat lunch.

She put her lunch in the microwave and went to the bathroom. When she returned, her lunch was ready. She

took it out and grabbed a clean fork. Abee set her lunch on
her desk and turned to look at her email.

For a few minutes, she focused on opening the
container without spilling it. Lunch was rice, grilled fish,
and some grilled vegetables. There was a little compartment
full of Ma'am's spicy jambalaya. Abee couldn't explain it,
but the spicy, warm food helped to ground her when she was
surrounded by blue flame.

She stuck her fork into a hot sausage and looked at
her email.

The first email was from Everett's cousin, the evil
Elaine Beauchamp.

Nearly every day, Elaine wrote Abee to tell her that
she was "an whore" or "a black banshee" or "a jezebel" or
something else. She used the "n" word to describe Abee in
every communication. Elaine had filed frivolous lawsuit
after dumb lawsuit against Abee.

Abee and Ma'am had discussed ways to curse the
girl, but when it came down to it, Abee didn't have that
kind of darkness inside her.

She hated that about herself.

Deep down, every time she heard from Elaine, Abee
couldn't help but feel grateful to the bogle who had helped
her face her fear of the woman. Sighing, Abee sent the bogle
a prayer of thanks and opened Elaine's email.

Tippi flapped her translucent wings. Abee looked at the sprite.

"Eat first," Tippi said.

"Good thinking," Abee said.

She made a little meal for Tippi in the top of her lunch container. For a few moments, they simply ate. Abee took a long drink of water before filling a tiny cup for Tippi. The sprite drank down her water.

"Okay," Abee said. "I'm ready."

Tippi nodded and flew to Abee's shoulder. Abee clicked to open the email.

"To whom it may concern: You may not be smart enough to . . ." the email started.

"Nope," Abee said. She jumped up from her seat. "I do not have time for that."

Tippi clapped her little hands.

"The hospital," Abee said to Tippi, "you know, the one my grandmother was in? It's like an hour from here. If Mom's nurse is here, I could go there and take a look around."

Abee saw Tippi's worried look.

"There are ghosts there," Tippi said.

"There are ghosts everywhere," Abee said.

"Not here or in the forest," Tippi said with a big smile.

"Well, you can stay here if it's too much," Abee said. "I will not love you less."

Abee nodded.

"I'm going to go and see what I can find," Abee said. "Maybe there are ghosts who know what happened to Nev. Get some juicy details for my paper."

"Seems reckless," Tippi said.

Abee didn't respond. Instead, she stuffed a few things into her backpack and used the restroom one last time. When Abee grabbed her backpack, Abee's Plott Hound, Goji, jumped down from her bed. Goji shook her head before racing Abee out the door. Abee and Goji took the wooden stairwell in a clumping and pounding flurry of steps. They reached the first floor and went into the living room, where Joanna's bed was located since she'd returned home.

Joanna's nurse, Makayla, scowled at Abee.

"Your mother was sleeping until you started down the stairs," Makayla said with a sniff.

Abee gave what she thought was a contrite look. Joanna's eyes shifted to look at Abee.

"If Mom was sleeping, why are you feeding her?" Abee asked.

Makayla snorted and shot Abee a dark look. The nurse held a spoonful of mashed yams in front of Joanna's mouth. Joanna's eyes flicked back to look at Makayla.

"Can you stay with mom until I get back?" Abee asked.

"I'll need to leave at my regular time," Makayla said.

"But you can stay with Mom," Abee said.

"Until my regular time," Makayla said in a tone that indicated that Abee was slow.

"Great," Abee said. "You get off at?"

"I need to leave here at six," Makayla said.

"I'll be back by then," Abee said. "Have you seen my Ma'am?"

"She has an important meeting in the city," Makayla said. "I'm sure she doesn't need to be disturbed by the likes of you."

Abee gave Makayla a long look. Makayla was only a year old than Abee, yet she acted like Abee was a child. Ma'am thought it was funny, but sometimes Abee wanted to wring Makayla's neck. If Makayla wasn't so good with Joanna, Abee would have fired her a long time ago.

Today, Abee wasn't going to give Makayla the satisfaction of getting her goat.

"Sure," Abee said. "I'll be back by then."

Abee turned over her wrist to look at her watch.

"I have enough time," Abee said.

"Where are you going?" Makayla asked.

"Kuhn Memorial Hospital," Abee said. "Vicksburg."

Joanna spit out the mouthful of food Makayla had just fed her. Joanna made a grunting sound.

"Now look what you've done," Makayla said. "She's upset."

Makayla stood up and stepped forward. Abee took a step back. Using her girth, Makayla pushed Abee toward the door.

"We'll see you when you get back," Makayla said and slammed the door in Abee's face.

Goji barked at the door. Abee shook her head at the nurse. A glance told her that Ma'am had taken her car to the city. Abee looked over to her 1964½ dark- green Mustang convertible. The car had been Everett's wedding present to her. Uncle Al had installed all the modern safety gear like airbags and good seatbelts. He'd even installed a seat belt in the back seat so that she could keep Goji safe.

Abee smiled every time she looked at the vehicle.

The car was beautiful, especially with the top down like it was now.

It was from Everett.

Sitting in the driver's seat, she reminded herself that Everett loved her. They would connect soon. He was missing her as much as she was missing him — at least that's what he said in every message and email.

She helped Goji into the backseat and snapped her in. Then she set her backpack into the foot well of the passenger seat and clipped her phone into the dash holder. Tippi flew in from the top and sat in the passenger seat.

"Everything is going to be okay," Abee said to herself.

Abee couldn't be sure if that was deep knowing or some kind of simple affirmation. Shaking her head at herself, she put in the address of the Kuhn Memorial Hospital and started the car. She started off toward the Mississippi River.

Turning on an audiobook about classical philosophy, Abee turned onto U.S. Route 65 and headed south. She loved driving her Mustang. Tippi happily rode in the wind on the edge of the windscreen. Remembering that she was more patient with the dead on a full stomach, she stopped at a fast-food restaurant in Richmond, Louisiana. She bought a few hamburgers with extra patties for Goji, a small fry for Tippi, and a large iced tea.

Back on the highway, she turned onto Interstate 20. She ate her burgers and laughed at Tippi as the tiny fairy ate the entire order of fries. They reached Vicksburg in no time.

Abee got off the highway at Halls Ferry Road. She had her first sense of dread when her Internet map service guided her onto Confederate Road. The road almost immediately became Mission 66. Mission 66 took her almost out of town. Her dread disappeared when she turned onto Martin Luther King Boulevard.

"How bad can it be?" Abee asked as they pulled into the driveway. "Look, the grass is mowed and everything."

"I don't like this," Tippi said. "We should wait for Ma'am."

"What could happen?" Abee asked.

Abee pulled the car next to the carport covering the entrance on the side of the front building. Her first impression was that this was a large property. From the maps, Abee knew that the building behind this building was shaped in the form of a cross. The front of the building had a grey cement façade that said "Kuhn Memorial State Hospital." The rest of the building was made from red brick. There was a white colored walkway that connected the two red-brick buildings. Tall trees and brush formed a thick forest on either side of the hospital. A maintained driveway went around the building and the water tower in the back.

A crowd of ghosts surrounded the car. Confederate soldiers, missing various body parts, roamed around mindlessly. Ghosts of Natchez Indians appeared out of nowhere. The indigenous men and women moved toward her. There were other ghosts — adults, babies, children. There was such a congregation of spirits that Abee knew she needed to do something.

There were few things more disgusting to Abee than spirits trapped in the world. Spirits should move onto the other side after death. That was the natural order of things.

The sheer number of trapped spirits indicated that something was very wrong here.

"Stay," Abee said to Goji. She pointed to Tippi. "Close your eyes and hide."

Knowing what Abee was about to do, Tippi nodded.

Abee hopped out of the Mustang. She flicked her right hand, and a round blue ball appeared. She grabbed the ball, and the flame grew in both directions. The blaze grew until it reached six feet. A blue flame blade formed on both ends. She and Ma'am discovered that she could make this spear when they were working with her blue flame. So far, she'd learned a few tricks.

Abee walked to the middle of the lawn. She stuck one end of the spear into the ground so the other blue fire blade faced up. She clapped her hands, and the blue flame shot up to create an opening to the other side. Abee put her fingers in her mouth and whistled.

"Hey!" Abee said. "Time to get out of here."

Unlike any other time she'd done this trick, the ghosts continued milling around. It was as if they had no idea she was talking to them.

"Hey! You! Faceless!" Abee yelled. "Time to meet your maker."

The faceless ghost of a Confederate soldier continued milling around.

"Okay," Abee said. "Have it your way."

Onto trick number two. She lifted the flaming blue spear and dropped it. This motion created a kind of vacuum. Ghosts were sucked up in the vacuum and sent on to the other side. It took a few minutes, but eventually, the area around the hospital was clear of the tortured departed souls.

"Fuck you, ghost hunters," Abee said after the last mindless spirit disappeared to the other side.

Abee picked up the spear and went back to her car. To her surprise, an apparition of a Natchez brave was standing next to the car. The Native American lowered his head in her direction.

"Not to me," Abee said. "I just wield the tools of the Mother of Sacred Fire."

The Natchez brave nodded. Abee opened her hand and tossed the blue flame spear into the air. It disappeared.

"I do not recommend that you go inside," the Natchez brave said. "It is dangerous to you, Abeegail Normal."

"Why?" Abee asked.

"The Doctor will try to enslave your soul, as he has your ancestor," the Natchez brave said.

"You mean there was a reason all those ghosts were here?" Abee asked.

"The Doctor kept them lost and locked in this location," the Natchez brave said.

"But not you?" Abee asked.

"I came a long way to assist you," the Natchez brave said. "I was called by your sacred flame. I send you blessings from the Mother."

Abee smiled.

"Blessings back to her," Abee said. "But I'm going inside."

"I cannot convince you to drop this task?" the Natchez brave asked.

"You cannot," Abee said. "When my grandmother was a child, she came here for help. What she got was not help. For all of my life, I thought she was just crazy. But when I read her file, I realized that her mental illness just might be from a soul split."

The Natchez brave scowled at her words. She took a breath and continued on.

"Part of my grandmother could be stuck here, causing her mental illness," Abee said. "If this 'doctor' is holding part of her soul hostage, I need to free her. And I can't leave all these souls here to . . . wander aimlessly. It affects the balance."

"Yes, I see your challenge," the Natchez brave said.

"Plus, I have a very small fairy who will protect me," Abee said.

Tippi poked her head out from under the seat. She flew up to look at the Natchez brave.

"And Goji the Goblin Hunter," Abi said.

Goji looked up at the Natchez brave.

"I am at your service until you no longer need me," the Natchez brave said.

"If you think I need your help, I am glad for it," Abee said. "What shall I call you?"

"My name is Lvlvpo'hv Uhtswe't," the Natchez brave said.

Abee wasn't sure why, but she was able to easily translate his name into "Strong Warrior." Abee nodded.

"What should I call you?" Abee repeated. "'Mr. Uhtswe't'? 'Lvlvpo'hv'?"

"You may call me . . ." the Natchez brave thought for a moment. He smiled. "Call me 'Lvl.'"

"'Level'?" Abee asked. "Or 'Lvl'?"

"'Level' sounds nice," the Natchez brave smiled. "Modern."

Abee nodded in understanding.

"This is Tippi." Abee gestured to the sprite.

The Natchez brave nodded to Tippi. In return, Tippi showered him with fairy lights. He grinned at her. Her lights brought curious sprites from the nearby forest. Afraid of the strangers, these sprites kept their distance and watched.

"We had these," Level gestured to Tippi, "when I was alive. We had great plans to capture them, but . . ."

The Natchez brave shook his head. Abee grinned.

"Me, too," Abee said. "I never caught one, either."

"What of this one?" Level said.

"She is my friend," Abee said.

Level nodded and smiled as if he found the whole thing amusing.

"This is Goji," Abee said. "She is a goblin hunter."

"A hunter of evil," Level nodded. "She is beautiful."

Level knelt down to Goji's level. The dog wagged her tail.

"What do you say we go find this 'doctor'?" Abee asked.

She bent over to unhook Goji, and the dog jumped out of the Mustang. She waited for Goji to go potty. She leaned down to place a protective barrier of blue flame around Goji. The dog shook herself but then looked up at Abi. Goji was ready to go.

"Ready?" Abee asked.

"I will follow you," Level said.

Ma'am pulled into the driveway and saw that Abee's 1964½ Mustang was gone. She grabbed her bag, locked her car, and went inside. As if she'd been waiting for Ma'am, Makayla was standing next to the front door.

"Makayla," Ma'am said as she took off her wrap and set down her bag.

"Ma'am, I don't know what to do," Makayla said. "Ms. Normal is in a right state."

"Joanna?" Ma'am asked. "What has happened?"

"She seemed fine, absolutely fine, until that Abee stomped down those stairs and disturbed her peace," Makayla said, "with her bird and that dog and whatever else. She is a menace. I forced her to leave."

"Where is Abee?" Ma'am asked.

"I don't know," Makayla said with an exaggerated shrug. "All I know is that Abee caused Ms. Normal much distress. You need to speak to that girl. She cannot be allowed to upset her mother at this crucial time in her healing."

Ma'am squinted at Makayla.

"What did Abee say?" Ma'am said, in a tone that demanded a response.

"She said that she was going to some hospital," Makayla said in a whiney tone. "That's all I know. Because Ms. Normal started spitting up her food and went into a right fit. I had to restrain her."

Ma'am gave Makayla a long look. After a moment, Ma'am took a breath.

"Why don't I take over from you?" Ma'am asked. Her voice shifted to soothing. "You've clearly had a rough afternoon."

"That is right," Makayla said. "I did not take this job to deal with sassy young ladies and out-of-control patients."

Makayla stood on her toes to put her face near Ma'am's.

"I am in demand," Makayla said. "I don't need to be treated like this!"

"Yes, I see," Ma'am said. "Why don't you take the rest of the afternoon off?"

Ma'am gave Makayla a kind smile. Makayla sniffed, grabbed her bag, and started toward the door.

"She'd better not be like this when I come back tomorrow," Makayla said as she went out the door. "That's all I'm saying."

The front door slammed. Ma'am scowled at the door. Ma'am went into the kitchen to turn on the kettle. She used the restroom and made some tea for Joanna. When she went into the room, she saw what Makayla meant by restraining Joanna.

Joanna was tied to her chair with a belt around her torso and the chair. She had tape around her wrists and the arms of the chair. Another belt was wrapped around Joanna's legs and the chair's front legs. Joanna's eyes were

CASEBOOK VOLUME 02,

Abee Normal, Paranormal Investigations   80
The case of Crazy as . . .

closed, and her head tipped to the side as if she'd been drugged.

Ma'am set the tea down on the table near Joanna and began humming an ancient song. With the first note of Ma'am's tune, Joanna began to revive. She snapped her fingers, and duct tape around her wrists and arms began to unwind.

Ma'am set the tea cup into Joanna's now-free hands. Joanna drank it down. Ma'am continued humming. She told the belt around Joanna's legs to unhook itself, which it did. The belt around Joanna's torso flew off with the effort to unhook.

Joanna fell forward. Ma'am caught her and pressed Joanna back into her chair. Joanna held the now-empty tea cup out to Ma'am.

Ma'am took the cup. She went into the kitchen to refill the tea. Joanna drank down the hot liquid and held the cup out again. Joanna and Ma'am went a few more rounds on this silent dance. Joanna set the cup down on the table.

"Where is Abee?" Ma'am asked.

Joanna's determination was apparent on her face. Her mouth screwed up. Her nose twitched, and her eyebrows dropped in focus.

"K-k-k," Joanna managed. She shook her head.

"Joanna, this is our Abee," Ma'am said. "I have put up with this nonsense because you need to get through this

Emery bullshit by your own will. But it's no longer about you. This is our Abee. I won't allow her to get lost in all of your self-flagellation."

Ma'am grabbed Joanna by the shoulders. Joanna's eyes locked with Ma'am's. Seconds turned to minutes. Minutes grew. Finally able to accept real help, Joanna allowed Ma'am to pour strength into her. Joanna took a breath and then another.

"Tell me," Ma'am demanded.

"K-k . . ." Joanna sighed. She clenched her fists and leaned forward with the effort. "Kuhn. To . . . h-hospital."

Ma'am reared back.

"How?" Ma'am asked. "Why?"

Joanna shook her head.

"Well, get yourself ready," Ma'am said. "We're going to save Abee."

"M-m-m-eee?" Joanna asked.

"Damn straight," Ma'am said. "You are her mother. It's time you got around to acting like it."

Expecting Joanna to balk, Ma'am gave Joanna a firm look. But Joanna only nodded.

"I . . . c-c-can . . ." Joanna said with a nod.

"Damn right, you can," Ma'am said.

Ma'am deposited Joanna in her wheelchair and went to get herself ready. She found Joanna on the toilet in the bathroom. Ma'am helped Joanna clean up and get back

into the wheelchair. Ma'am pushed the wheelchair to the
bag she'd packed. She put the bag in Joanna's lap, and they
went out the door.

"Di-i-i-d Abee . . . married?" Joanna asked.

"Everett," Ma'am said. "They love each other. She's
wanted to marry him since she was ten years old."

Joanna nodded.

Ma'am looked at Joanna to see if she had something
else to say, but Joanna didn't respond. Ma'am opened the
passenger door of her baby-blue 1952 Chrysler Imperial and
pulled the wheelchair up to it. She left Joanna to figure out
how to get inside. Ma'am went to drop her bag and a set of
tools in the trunk. She set her bag of snacks and tea on the
back seat. When she looked up, Joanna had managed to get
into the passenger seat.

Ma'am took the wheelchair and stuck it in the wide
back seat.

"C-c-could you . . ." Joanna started. She swallowed
hard. "I need cr-cr-cr . . ."

Ma'am raised her eyebrows.

"You want your crutches?" Ma'am said.

Joanna nodded. Ma'am went back into the house.
She stuck a container jambalaya in the microwave and went
to find Joanna's forearm crutches. She grabbed the
container, a napkin and fork, and left the house.

"Eat this," Ma'am said. "All of it."

She dumped the stew, napkin, and fork in Joanna's lap and put the crutches away. Ma'am got into the driver's seat. Joanna took a few tentative bites of stew before consuming it all in a matter of minutes. She leaned forward as her stomach cramped.

"Hungry," Joanna said.

"I bet," Ma'am said.

"Water?" Joanna asked.

Ma'am took a water bottle out of her bag. Joanna took a drink.

"Tea?" Joanna asked.

Ma'am took out a thermal travel mug. Joanna took a long drink.

"Th . . .ankk," Joanna said.

"I love you, Joanna," Ma'am said.

Ma'am looked at Joanna, and Joanna put her hand on her chest.

"Ready?" Ma'am asked.

"Re'd . . ." Joanna said with a nod.

Ma'am started the car and took off down the lane.

Tippi landed on Abbi's shoulder. They walked under the carport. Abee stopped walking. The building no longer had doors. From where she stood, she could see into what had been the lobby. The sheetrock on the walls was crumbling. Wires hung down from the ceiling. Loose linoleum tiles lay around the floor in a haphazard fashion.

She saw something else.

She wasn't sure what.

Ever since her "transformation," she'd begun to see, hear, and smell things that she didn't quite understand. Right now, she could see the light around the door shimmer, almost the color and consistency of the reflection off a soap bubble.

"Goji, what do you see?" Abee asked.

Tippi flew down to stand on the dog's head. Goji looked up at Abee.

As clear as if she were seeing it herself, she received an image of what Goji was seeing. Goji saw a grayish barrier over the door of the building. In Goji's vision, the barrier was not translucent but made of a gray textured material that was vacuum suctioned onto the building.

"I think I'm going to need this," Abee said, to herself.

She bounced a ball of blue fire until it became a spear of blue flame.

She felt a shiver of fear go through her. Her rage and impotence at her own situations pushed the fear aside. If there was something she could do here, she was going to do it.

She held the spear at her side, level to the ground, so that one of the points was out in front of her. Level, the Natchez brave, moved to her left side. She looked at him, and he nodded. Goji and Tippi were on her right.

With nothing left to say, she stepped to the door. The point of the spear pierced the membrane, creating a hole.

They stepped through the membrane and into the lobby.

"Oh," Tippi said.

The lobby had transformed into what it had looked like when this was a functioning hospital. As if they'd been transported into the 1980s, the hospital lobby was bustling with people. Nurses rushed from here and there. Patients patiently waited for someone to help them.

And . . .

"Do you see it?" Abee asked. "Both worlds."

"I only see the busy lobby," Level said.

"It's like being inside your motion pictures," Tippi whispered. "Everyone is here, but they cannot see us or interact."

"Goji?" Abee asked.

Goji looked up at Abee, and she saw that the lobby had not transformed for Goji. The dog was still seeing the dilapidated front entry of a ruin of a hospital.

"Look at the tip of the spear," Abee said. "Just in front of the blade."

There was a round hole, about two feet wide, in the vision that showed the lobby as it was today. Abee moved the spear around. Pointing the spear at the ceiling, she saw that the ceiling was falling in, stained with moisture from leaks, and moldy. The walls were peeling and falling in.

In the vision, they saw a nurse sitting behind an old computer. She looked up at them and smiled.

"May I help you?" the nurse in the vision asked.

When the tip of the spear pointed at the front desk, they saw the dilapidated desk. No one was sitting there. Not even a ghost.

"That's what Goji sees," Abee said.

Fascinated, they looked around the room from the vision to the port hole into reality.

"Excuse me," a man's voice said.

They'd been so focused on this bizarre experience of seeing two realities that they weren't paying attention to their surroundings. Abee looked up to see a doctor moving toward her. She glanced at Level.

"That's him," Level said.

She pointed the spear at him. The creature in front of them was not a spirit. The Doctor was a human skeleton covered in tight, cracking skin. The body looked dehydrated, as if all moisture had been sucked out of it.

There was a filthy, old lab coat hanging off the shoulders of this ghoul. On top of a skeletal neck, its shriveled skull held in bulging eyes, which flicked back and forth in an unnatural way. The creature's head held a few wisps of dark hair.

"Is there something I can help you with?" the man said.

He took a step forward. Bits of skin flaked off his exposed skin in a kind of cloud.

"Who are you?" Abee asked.

"I am the Doctor," the man said.

"I see," Abee said.

In the vision, she saw the nurses looking very deferentially in his direction. When she swung the spear to where they appeared to be, there was nothing there. Not even a specter or a memory of a ghost.

This "vision" was a hallucination that she was creating in her own brain. She glanced at Tippi. The tiny fairy was experiencing the same hallucination. She glanced at Level. He seemed confused.

"What do you see?" Abee said in a low tone.

"It is very . . . fuzzy as if . . ." Level swallowed hard. "We are looking through a cloud or mist. Something is confusing our minds and vision."

Abee turned to look at the Doctor. In the vision, the Doctor was a strapping man, in the height of his health and power. He had a full head of thick black hair, dark eyes, and a set of white teeth. His skin was white, and his laboratory coat was bright white.

Through the portal off the tip of her blue blaze spear, the Doctor looked like a dried-up corpse.

Tippi flew up to Abee's shoulder next to her ear.

"This is complicated magic," Tippi said quietly so that only Abee could hear.

"Demonic," Level said in a low tone.

"You have made our patients uncomfortable," the Doctor said.

"You're sure that's him?" Abee asked under her breath.

"Hv-vh'." Level affirmed that this was the "Doctor" he'd spoken about previously.

"You need to leave this place," the Doctor said. "Immediately."

"We're here to release the souls you have trapped here," Abee said in a voice that was stronger than she felt.

"You will not remove my patients from my care," the Doctor said. "These patients need my help. I will never abandon them."

Tippi sucked in a breath.

The hall behind the doctor filled with the souls of those caught here. There were hundreds of souls here. There were souls of elderly people, children, even a few infants stood in the hallway. More than anything, there were hundreds of souls of young women like Abee's grandmother.

"I'm here to get my grandmother," Abee said. "Alicia Harris. She no longer needs your help."

The Doctor's malevolent laugh sent a shiver of fear through Abee.

"I will not leave without her," Abee said.

"Who said that you would leave?" the Doctor said. "Your grandmother is here? Mental illness runs in families. You are obviously a liar like your grandmother. Having hallucinations?"

The Doctor chortled.

"There's something in the air," Abee said to Tippi and Level. "Tippi? Can you get . . .?"

In a flash, Abee's mouth was covered with a high-quality respirator held on by plastic straps around her head. She glanced at Tippi. The tiny fairy was wearing a high-quality respirator as well. Abee's vision was slightly distorted. Her hand touched her face. Tippi had given her protective glasses. The tiny fairy was wearing protective glasses, too. Even Goji was wearing his dog goggles and a dog respirator.

"Level?" Abee asked.

"I do not breathe air," Level said. "If this is airborne, you should begin to see what I see."

"A kind of fog?" Abee asked.

Level grunted.

The Doctor watched their interaction with a kind of detached scientific interest.

"You done?" the Doctor asked in such a way as to assert his dominance. "I'd hate to interrupt."

Abee did not respond.

"I didn't think so," the Doctor said with a sniff.

He turned in place and started walking down the hallway.

"This way," the Doctor said. "You will follow me."

Abee glanced at Level and then at Tippi.

"Magic?" Abee asked.

"Demonic," Level repeated.

Tippi nodded. Abee made a movement with her hand, and Goji moved out in front of them.

"Are you coming?" the Doctor asked.

They started forward. As they walked down the hallway, Abee could feel the ghosts watching her. A five-or six-year old child appeared at their side. The girl was wearing clothing from of the 1970s. Her skin was milk-chocolate brown, and her eyes were light. Her dark hair was combed into two puffy ponytails on the top of her head.

"Wanna play?" the child asked.

Abee stopped walking. The Doctor was out ahead of them. In a moment, he would turn down a hallway and likely be lost forever. Abee looked around her. She was surrounded by ghosts. She looked down at the little girl.

"Alicia?" Abee asked.

The girl broke into a big smile.

"How'd you know?" the girl asked.

Abee just smiled at the girl.

"Goji," Abee said to get her dog's attention. "Watch."

Abee commanded Goji to watch for danger. Goji sat down so that she could see every angle of the hallway.

The longer they stood in this hallway, the more ghosts showed up. Abee scanned the crowd. There were a lot of young women here.

"Why are you here?" Abee asked.

"We can't leave," a voice from the middle of the pack of ghosts said.

"Who said that?" Abee asked. "Show yourself, or I will not respond."

The ghost of a 16 or 17 year-old African-American woman pushed her way through the crowd. When she stepped out in front of the others, Tippi gasped.

Abee felt like she was looking into a photo album. The young woman in front of her was most certainly her grandmother.

"Alicia?" Abee asked.

The young woman nodded.

CASEBOOK VOLUME 02,
Abee Normal, Paranormal Investigations
The case of Crazy as . . .

92

"Why are there two of you?" Abee asked.

The apparition simply looked at Abee.

"You don't know?" Abee asked.

"I feel like I *should* know, but . . ." Alicia shrugged.

Abee stopped talking when she saw a woman standing near the wall. One of Abee's classmates had given a presentation on "Civil War Nurses" because one of her ancestors was a Sister of Mercy nun who'd been pressed into service of the Confederacy during the civil war. The woman Abee had noticed was wearing a nurse's uniform from the Civil War. The nurse bore more than a passing resemblance to Abee's classmate.

"You there." Abee pointed to the nurse.

The nurse looked up and pointed to herself.

"Yes, you," Abee said. "Sister? Can you come forward?"

The ghost nodded and moved in Abee's direction. As she moved through the crowd, it was clear that this nurse had the respect of the other souls trapped here.

"How may I help you?" the nurse asked.

The nurse's name tag said, "Sister Agatha Nevins." The woman who'd given the presentation in Abee's class was named, "Destynee Nevins." This must be her classmate's ancestor. Abee gave the woman a warm smile.

"I am Abee Normal. I am here to free the souls who are trapped here," Abee said. "I'm wondering if you can tell me *why* these people are stuck here."

She tried to take the tone of someone talking to a nurse in a functioning hospital. The woman smiled at Abee.

"What would you like me to tell you?" the nurse asked.

"Why are these souls stuck here?" Abee tried again.

"What would you like me to tell you?" the nurse repeated.

Frustrated, Abee scowled. There was nothing Abee wanted to do more than to get her grandmother and get the heck out of here. This ghost seemed to be playing games.

"I believe she's asking you which story you would like to hear about why they are here," Level said.

Abee remembered that many of the Sisters of Mercy were actually prisoners of the Confederate Army. She paused for a moment while she thought.

"Do you know the true reason these spirits are trapped here?" Abee asked.

"I believe so," the nurse said.

"Would you tell me the truth?" Abee asked. "I will do everything in my power to set you and the rest of these people free. If I am unable to set you free, I know someone who is your descendent. I can lead her through the process of freeing you."

Sister Nevins scanned Abee's face.

"Help me," Abee said. "I *will* help you and the others."

Sister Nevins gave a quick nod.

"Follow me," Sister Nevins said.

Sister Nevins took off down the hallway. Abee and Goji ran to keep up with her. Sister Nevins stopped at the doorway of a ward. Sister Nevins nodded inside the room.

There were hundreds of Civil War soldiers on this ward. Even through the respirator, the smell of the ward was enough to cause Abee to back up. She felt Goji press her head against Abee's knee. Tippi flew up to Abee's shoulder.

"Do you see this?" Abee asked.

"Yes," Tippi said.

Level nodded. Goji looked up at Abee.

"Do you see the doctor?" Sister Nevins asked.

Abee scanned the room until she saw a man standing along the wall. He was giving instructions to two nurses. Abee nodded to Sister Nevins.

"Do you see the other?" Sister Nevins pointed to a man.

Lying on a cot, the man stared at the doctor with unmasked rage.

"Is that . . .?" Abee leaned forward to get a better look.

The man in the bed was "The Doctor," the apparition who had trapped all of these souls here.

"He felt that the doctor and nurses were not doing their best for the Confederate soldiers," Sister Nevins said. "So many died. Most injuries were severe. Life threatening. There was so much death that . . . There wasn't anything anyone could do. But he felt that anyone paying attention to anyone other than Confederate soldiers was stealing from the Confederacy. When he died, he took up residency here. He has exerted his malice and rage upon any soul that was available to him."

Sister Nevins nodded.

"He was buried here?" Abee asked.

"They had to bury men here at the hospital," Sister Nevins said. "Every form of disease was rampant, especially during the siege. The men had to be buried here in mass graves."

"Really?" Abee asked.

Sister Nevins nodded.

"It was a common practice," Sister Nevins said.

"Huh," Abee said.

Abee thought for a moment before she turned to Sister Nevins.

"Now we know how he got here," Abee said.

Sister Nevins nodded to Abee and started to move off.

"Why are there so many girls here?" Abee asked.

"There was a long history of doctors sexually assaulting and torturing girls and young women at this hospital," Sister Nevins said in a matter-of-fact tone. "These assaults split off portions of the girls' souls."

"These portions of souls were trapped by the Doctor?" Abee asked.

"Exactly," Sister Nevins said.

"Why would anyone want to do that?" Abee asked. "I mean, you're saying that he didn't assault the women or torture them. He only trapped their poor tortured souls."

"For power," Sister Nevins said. "He wanted complete power over them. You must know that traumatized people are susceptible to giving up their power."

"My Ma'am says that's why people are tortured," Abee said. "So they give up their will."

"She is correct," Sister Nevins said.

"Could these women be alive?" Abee asked. "I mean, if he only took a piece of their soul, then . . ."

"Some of them are still alive — or were," Sister Nevins said. "Weren't you looking for your grandmother? She is alive, yes?"

Abee nodded.

"She left pieces of her soul here," Sister Nevins said.

"She's been diagnosed as a schizophrenic," Abee said.

"I imagine many of these women have been as well," Sister Nevins said.

"And the others?" Abee asked. "How did the rest of them get here?"

"He took as many as he could," Sister Nevins said.

Abee nodded.

"Thank you," Abee said.

"You will never be able to break his hold over our souls," Sister Nevins said. "It is simply impossible."

Sister Nevins gave Abee a slight nod and floated away.

Trying to take in all that she learned, Abee stood still. She wished that she had waited for Ma'am. There was no question in her mind that Ma'am would know exactly what to do.

"What if that's true?" Abee asked out loud. "What if I cannot break the hold he has over these souls?"

Abee tried to think it through. She glanced at her five-year-old grandmother and her teenaged grandmother. She could not leave them here with him.

She would not leave them here with him.

The more she thought, the more confused she became. Every time a solution to her problem came into focus, it drifted away. She thought and thought and thought.

Without warning, Goji bumped into her.

Abee stumbled and nearly fell. When she got up, she realized that she'd been standing in place for a long time.

"What's going on?" Abee asked Level.

"We have not been sure," Level said. "You have been staring into space for a long time."

"It must be a trick of the Doctor," Abee said.

"You are under his spell?" Level gave her a look of concern.

"I keep getting an idea, and then it . . ." Abee made a "pfft" sound, as if the idea went up in smoke. "I . . ."

Abee felt herself drift off again.

"Under his spell . . ." Abee mumbled.

She held the point of her blue flame spear over her head. Looking up, she allowed the blue flame to wash over her entire body. After a moment, she dropped the sword to her side. She stroked Goji's soft ears, and she looked at Level and then at Tippi.

"Got it," Abee said.

Nodding, Abee went back into the ghost ward where the Civil War soldiers were being treated. She stopped a nurse. The woman was old. Her skin was so white and translucent that Abee thought she could see the woman's heart beat in her veins. She had a kind look, pale-blue eyes, and a kind feel about her. Abee felt an instant like for the woman.

"May I help you, dear?" the Sister asked.

"Where do you bury the dead?" Abee asked.

"Why do you wish to know, child?" The Sister's kind look brought tears to Abee's eyes.

"I . . ." Abee started.

"A death in your family," the Sister said with a nod. "I understand. Thousands have died since this siege began. Every family is missing loved one."

The Sister gave a rueful shake of her head. She pointed to the apparition of a Native boy. He was working on the ward. He stared at Level and then turned back to the Sister.

"Show them where the men are buried," the Sister said to the boy. Turning back to Abee, the Sister said, "I am afraid that we cannot tell you exactly where your beloved might be buried."

"How is it organized?" Abee asked.

"By date," the Sister said. "The boy will show you."

Abee's eyes drifted to the dying soldier she knew to be the "Doctor."

"What is today's date?" Abee asked.

"May 30, 1863," the Sister said. She leaned into Abee. "I believe you're looking for July 2nd."

The Sister winked at Abee and drifted away. Smiling, Abee watched her go. She looked back at Level, Tippi, and then Goji. She held out her hand, and Goji put her muzzle into Abee's hand.

The boy spoke in Natchez for a moment. Level listened intently and then turned to Abee.

"He says that he will show us where the bodies are buried," Level said. "He will not go to the graves."

Abee gave Level a questioning look.

"It is common for our people to have a reverence for death and the dead," Level said simply.

"And that means?" Abee asked.

"We don't go to grave sites," Level said.

"Okay," Abee said. "Can he find a specific one?"

Level asked the boy a question. They spoke back and forth for a while. Abee was mostly able to follow the conversation. When they stopped talking, Level turned to Abee.

"The men are buried together," Level said. "There is no single grave site."

Abee nodded.

"Lead on," Abee said to the boy.

The apparition of the Natchez boy took off down the corridor. With Goji out in front, Abee jogged to keep up with him. The Natchez boy went through the connection between hospitals. He headed out across the first floor and then abruptly turned left. He ran until they reached a back door. There was a heavy iron chain around the door mechanism and a big key padlock.

Luckily, Abee had been learning to pick locks by watching videos on the Internet. She practiced late at night when her mind was crazy and she couldn't sleep. She'd gotten fairly good at it.

Abee took her picks out of the pocket of her jeans.

This lock took her a while because the mechanism was rusty. But she was through it soon enough. She pulled the chain off the lock.

She pressed the door open. The forest appeared right outside the door to the building. Goji, with Tippi on her back, started out of the building. Abee stepped out of the building behind Goji.

She had expected the Natchez boy to run out ahead again. When he didn't, she turned to look at him. The apparition of the Natchez boy was pressed against the membrane they'd seen when they'd entered the building. He could not leave.

"Shit," Abee said.

Level spoke to the boy in Natchez. The boy gestured and pointed. Level nodded that he understood.

"We'll free you," Abee said.

Abee's hand flew to her heart. In response, the boy put his hand flat against the membrane. Abee gave him a sad look and then turned to Level.

"Any ideas?" Abee asked.

"He says the graves are over there," Level said, pointing to the overgrown forest in front of them.

Standing at the edge of the forest, Abee peered into the dim light. She saw only deciduous trees and scrub brush.

"Where?" Abee asked.

"Yes, that's the problem," Level said. "He said that they were here."

Level gestured around the trees.

"These trees probably weren't here when he came to the hospital," Abee said.

"It is likely," Level said.

Tippi flew up so that she was at Abee's eyesight. Before Abee could say anything, Tippi flew into the forest.

"Tippi!" Abee yelled after her friend.

"She is a woodland creature," Level said.

"She is not from here," Abee said. "They have a complicated monarchy. Tippi is from California. She was able to live in the forest by my house because her Princess married a Prince of my forest. Her presence here could be seen as an act of war!"

Worried, Level, Abee, and Goji stood at the edge of the forest.

"Oh, Tippi," Abee whispered.

As if called by her words, a male sprite appeared.

"Abee Normal," the male sprite said. He gave a deep bow to Abee. "You and Goji the Goblin Hunter are well known to us. You are welcome."

"Where is Tippi?" Abee asked.

"She is visiting with her relatives," the male sprite said. "She should be to you shortly."

Abee gave the forest another worried look before giving her full attention to the male sprite.

"I am Alistai," the male sprite said. "I have come to take you to what you seek."

"This is . . ." Abee gestured to the apparition of the Natchez warrior.

"Lvlvpo'hv Uhtswe't," he said.

"Lvlvpo'hv Uhtswe't," the male sprite said with a respectful bow. "At your service."

"Alistai," Level said with a bow of his head.

The male sprite grinned at Level and then looked at Abee.

"I must say that meeting Abee Normal is a great honor," Alistai said.

"We are pleased to make your acquaintance as well," Abee said. "Can you help us find where they buried people in the Civil War?"

"There were a lot of people buried at that time," Alistai said. "There was the big war, of course. There was also disease — Spanish flu, yellow fever. They couldn't get the bodies in the ground fast enough."

Abee winced. This was going to be harder than she thought.

"Luckily for you, your friend Alistai the sprite was here when these human remains went into the ground," Alistai said with a wide grin.

"We are looking for a specific one," Abee said.

"Yes," Alistai said.

"We've been told that he may have died on July 2, 1863," Abee said.

"I'm afraid that is not of much help," Alistai said. "Your calendar is different from our calendar."

"What is today's date in your calendar?" Abee asked.

Alistai gave the date. Abee squinted.

"Months?" Abee asked.

"We have nearly a thousand," Alistai said primly. "They are of varying lengths depending on the season and the royal history and . . ."

"Okay," Abee said. "Okay."

She looked at Level.

"Any ideas?" Abee asked.

"Will you take Abee to the human remains from during the large battle around this city?" Level asked.

"You're not going?" Abee asked out of the side of her mouth.

"I will not go to graves," Level said.

Abee nodded. He'd said that before.

"Why don't I show you what is here?" Alistai asked.

"Lead on," Abee said.

Alistai flew up to Abee's sight line and began to fly at an easy pace. Abee followed right behind him. Just a few feet from the hospital, they'd lost sight of the hospital. The forest was close and the light dim. Feeling Abee's discomfort, Goji moved close to her.

And then Alistai was gone.

She spun in place. The male sprite was gone.

She had been tricked by this forest's sprite population. She'd walked right into their trap. They had used this Alistai to bring her into the forest, where she was lost.

Abee sighed.

The forest was not very big. Her logical mind told her that she could easily walk out of the forest. She knew the legends about sprites. It didn't matter how big the forest was. If a sprite wanted you to be lost, you were lost. There was nothing you could do about it. Any action you took would only lead to you being more lost.

She didn't dare move for fear of getting injured. This was a kind of prison that sprites put people and animals into. Any movement from this site could bring about the end of her and Goji's life.

Her heart nearly broke.

"Oh, Tippi," Abee whispered. Her heart welled with longing for her Ma'am. "Ma'am, I'm sorry."

She was so frustrated with herself and sick about being lost that she simply sat down. Goji climbed onto her lap.

"Abee!"

She heard her name called in what sounded like her mother Joanna's voice.

"Abee!"

Abee started to cry. Her mother was sick. These horrible sprites were mocking her by having her mother call her name.

"Abeegail!"

Goji licked her face. When Abee put her arm around her dog, she saw that she was still holding the spear in her hand. She jammed a point into the earth and shot a tower of fire to the sky.

If Ma'am ever came looking for her, she would see her flame.

"Joanna!" Ma'am's voice said. "Look!"

There was a general rustling not far from where Abee was lost. Convinced it was a cruel sprite joke, Abee pressed her face into Goji's fur and cried.

Abee felt arms on her shoulders. She turned her head to look and saw her mother.

"Mom?" Abee asked.

The bottom of Joanna's dress was covered in mud. The pegs of her forearm crutches were filthy. But her face was beautiful.

"Oh, Abee — it's just another hallucination," Abee said.

She closed her eyes and pressed her face into Goji's fur.

"Abeegail Normal," Joanna said.

"It's okay," Ma'am said.

Abee felt someone kneel down to her. Abee looked up to see Ma'am's face.

"Ma'am?" Abee asked. "How will I know it's you?"

"Joanna?" Ma'am asked.

There was a silence for a moment, and then Joanna started rapping.

"Man, Let's go," Joanna said. "Hey, Fif"

She waited.

"That's where you're supposed to say 'Yeah'," Joanna said. "How can I sing 'Jimmy Crack Corn' without you as Fifty Cent?"

"It's 'Fiddy' Cent," Abee said.

She turned her tear-streaked face to look at her mother. When Abee was five, Joanna had gone as the

American rapper Eminem, and Abee had gone as Fifty Cent for Halloween. They knew all of their raps together and sang them on request.

"Mama?" Abee asked.

"I would get down there to hug you, but I'd never get up," Joanna said.

Ma'am held her hand out, and Abee took it. Ma'am pulled Abee to standing. Abee stepped into her Ma'am's embrace. Joanna put her arms around both of them.

Abee couldn't help but cry with relief.

Ma'am let go.

"Let's give her some air," Ma'am said. She looked Abee in the eye. "What's happening?"

"Tippi went to get help from the sprites, but they led me here, and . . ." Abee said. "I'm locked in lost."

"We found you," Ma'am said. "That should break the spell."

Ma'am nodded her head toward the hospital.

"What's happening in there?" Ma'am asked. "Why did you come here?"

Abee explained about her school project. She told Ma'am about getting her grandmother's records and Alicia's assault at the desegregation rally. She told Ma'am about going inside the hospital and the membrane. She even remembered to tell Ma'am about Level.

"'Level' — really?" Ma'am asked. "He let you call him that?"

"He said it was 'modern,'" Abee said.

Grinning at Abee, Ma'am shook her head.

Abee continued her story about the Doctor and the trapped souls. She told them about the pieces of her grandmother's soul. She spoke of wanting to help the spirits trapped in the hospital but only making a mess out of everything by getting trapped herself.

Ma'am let Abee cry for a while.

Then, Abee realized that Ma'am was letting her cry. She looked up at Ma'am.

"You done?" Ma'am asked. "Because we can sit here in the dirt and cry some more."

Abee chuckled. Joanna laughed, which made Ma'am laugh.

"Stay," Ma'am said to Goji.

She stepped away from Abee and clapped her hands.

"I love it when she does this," Joanna said in Abee's ear.

"You knew?" Abee whispered back.

Joanna nodded.

Ma'am shot them a hard look.

"I command the release of the sprite, Tippi," Ma'am said. "Release her unharmed, and I will *try* to forget this incident. Fail to release her and . . ."

CASEBOOK VOLUME 02,
Abee Normal, Paranormal Investigations
The case of Crazy as . . .

110

Tippi appeared in front of Ma'am. Tippi's little face was red and wet with tears. She fluttered around like a dying insect until Abee caught her. Tippi sobbed in Abee's hand. To comfort the sprite, Abee tucked her into the pocket of her shirt. Tippi wrapped her wings around herself and nestled down at the bottom of the pocket.

"Now," Ma'am said. "You realize that Abee carries the Sacred Flame. With a flick of her hand, she can exterminate every sprite in this entire forest."

"I can?" Abee asked in a low tone.

Ma'am gave her an affirming nod.

"This is why she was imprisoned." Alistai, the male sprite Abee had dealt with before, appeared in front of Ma'am. "She is too immature to wield such a weapon."

"That's the sprite," Abee said. "The one who said he would help me."

"Abee is a child," Ma'am said. "You have betrayed the trust of a child. That is against the International Code of Sprites."

"She has been through her transition," Alistai said with a sniff.

"Abee?" Ma'am said. "Blast this forest. You can start with this one."

Unsure of exactly what she was supposed to do, Abee pointed the spear at the sprite.

"Whoa! Whoa!" the sprite said. He put his hands up. "Wait! Just wait a minute."

"Why should I?" Abee asked. "You lied to me. Tricked me. Hurt my friend Tippi! Imprisoned me in 'lost!'"

"What's a little fun among friends?" Alistai asked.

Abee felt Tippi shiver in her pocket.

"What if I just show you what you're looking for?" Alistai asked.

"I am still bringing this before the council," Ma'am said.

"Yes!" Alisitai brightened. "But you can also say that I helped you and Abee Normal right a wrong. Saved her grandmother and all of that."

"Show me where we need to go first," Ma'am said.

"The human bodies are buried all throughout this space and the forest on the other side," Alistai said. "Abee Normal said that you are looking for someone from 1863, human years."

"You know human calendar?" Abee asked, her temper starting to flare.

To his credit, Alistai actually looked a little guilty. Ma'am growled at his look, and he yelped as if he'd been stung.

"If that is what she said, then that's what we need," Ma'am said.

"That grave is particularly confusing," Alistai said. "There was a battle for the city. The graves are full of soldiers from both sides as well as Native peoples. Women. Children. There was an epidemic which killed thousands during the siege."

"You're saying that the grave we want is crowded," Ma'am said.

"I didn't ask you what was in the grave," Abee said. "Just where it was."

Ma'am nodded to give emphasis to Abee's words.

"Why should we believe this liar?" Abee asked with an angry sniff.

"Good question," Ma'am said. "You do a lot of talking and very little showing."

The tiny sprite took off flying. Goji went after the sprite. Ma'am was on Goji's heels. Abee grabbed her spear and helped Joanna along. They headed back toward the hospital and then along the side of the original hospital.

"You will find what you're looking for here," Alistai said. He started to go.

"I did not release you," Ma'am said. She pointed at the sprite. "You stay."

Goji sat down. Ma'am grinned at the dog and turned to Abee.

"What are we looking for?" Ma'am said.

"There's a living corpse inside who is holding traumatized souls captive," Abee said.

"Including my mama's?" Joanna asked.

"Five-year-old and a teenager," Abee said. "I thought that I could burn his remains. That would release him from this world as well as all of those he's held captive."

"What will happen to them?" Ma'am asked.

"I didn't think that far," Abee said. She scrunched up her face. "Can you . . .?"

"Just do it like we've practiced," Ma'am said. "You know how. You just don't know to do it now."

"Okay," Abee said. "That works."

Ma'am turned back to the male sprite.

"You will find the corpse Abee Normal is looking for," Ma'am said.

"I won't do it," Alistai said.

"He is in league with the Doctor," Tippi stuck her head out of Abee's pocket to say. "He is corrupt."

Tippi's little scared voice enraged Abee.

"Do you know who you're fucking with?" Abee asked.

She allowed her rage to rise. When Joanna jumped back, Abee knew that she was covered with blue flame. Abee pointed her spear at the sprite.

The tiny fairy yelped and recoiled with fear.

"Bring up the corpse," Abee said. She felt the blue fire come out her eyes. "Now."

Alistai snapped his fingers, and the ground began to rumble. Joanna started to tip over, but Ma'am held her upright.

The dirt began to shake and move. There was a pulsing from under the ground.

In the hospital behind them, they heard screaming and yelling. The door to the hospital slammed open. The Doctor flew out of the hospital.

The ground parted, and the remains of a Confederate soldier rose above the soil.

Abee pointed her spear at the remains. As she'd practiced with Ma'am, blue flame shot out of the end of the spear. The flame encompassed the remains.

The Doctor screamed with rage and pain. For a moment, it seemed like the fire wasn't going to do anything. The Doctor continued in their direction.

Suddenly, the apparition stopped coming toward them. He looked surprised.

There was a popping sound. A puff of smoke appeared where he'd been floating.

"Look," Joanna said reverentially.

Souls began to rise out of the hospital. They stood in silent revelry, watching the souls of those caught in the Doctor's clutches return to their living hosts or fade to the other side. Abee looked up to see a general din on the other side.

The souls who finally made it home were celebrated by a host of angels, friends, and family.

Abee grinned. Ma'am put her arm around Abee's shoulder.

"Nice," Ma'am said.

Letting go of Abee, Ma'am turned to see that the male sprite, Alistai, was gone.

"Where is the sprite?" Ma'am asked.

A tiny sprite military officer appeared.

"We have arrested him," said the sprite military officer with a lot of medals on the front of his uniform. "We were unable to do that when he was under the spell of that human. We have him in custody. We will be in touch for his trial."

"Thank you," Ma'am said.

She nodded to the sprite military officer. He disappeared.

"Well," Ma'am said.

"Let's go home!" Joanna said.

Abee grinned at her mother. They started toward the cars. They were almost to the car when Ma'am's cell phone rang. Ma'am stopped to answer it.

Abee opened her car door to let Goji in. Joanna stood between Abee and Ma'am.

"Yes," Ma'am said. "This is she."

There was a long pause as whoever was on the other end of the line spoke.

"I see," Ma'am said. "Of course. I'll be right there."

"What was that?" Joanna asked.

"That was your mother," Ma'am said. "She told the hospital that she's ready to come home now. They wanted to know if we would come to get her."

Ma'am looked at Abee and then at Joanna.

"What do you think?" Ma'am asked.

"Let's bring her home!" Joanna said.

Ma'am just grinned at Abee.

"You take Joanna home," Ma'am said. "Would you mind calling Al along the way? I'm sure he'd like to be there when she gets home."

Abee nodded. Shaking her head and grinning, Ma'am walked to her vehicle. She opened the door of the baby-blue car and looked at Abee.

"You did good, Abee," Ma'am said.

"Before or after I got held hostage?" Abee asked. She gave her Ma'am a grin.

"The whole thing," Ma'am said. "I'll see you at home."

Abee made sure that Goji had a long drink of water. She offered some water to Tippi, but Tippi wouldn't come out of her pocket.

"Would you mind if we . . .?" Joanna started.

"Are you okay?" Abee asked.

"I have to pee," Joanna said. "I drank about three gallons of your Ma'am's tea, and now . . ."

Abee laughed. She clipped Goji into the back and got in the car. Setting her cell phone in its holder, Abee turned around and drove out of the Kuhn Memorial State Hospital complex.

"They're going to tear this place down soon," Abee said.

"The sooner the better," Joanna said. "You think we should tell them about the bodies buried in the forest?"

"Probably," Abee said with a laugh.

Turning onto Martin Luther King Boulevard, Abee stopped at the nearest gas station so that Joanna could use the facilities. She walked to the liquor store next door and bought a tiny bottle of cheap bourbon and a paper cup. At the car again, Abee poured the bourbon into the cup.

"Tippi?" Abee asked.

Tippi looked out of Abee's pocket. Unable to resist the bourbon, Tippi flew to the cup and drank deeply. Abee called her Uncle Al while she waited for Tippi to finish and Joanna to reappear. He hung up on her because he was weeping uncontrollably.

"Ready?" Abee asked as Joanna got in the car.

Tippi flew back to Abee's pocket.

"For anything," Joanna said.

They started toward home. They'd been on the highway for about ten minutes before Tippi climbed out of Abee's pocket. When she took her place in the wind at the top of the windscreen in the wind, Abee smiled.

Everything seemed like it was going to be okay.

When she pulled into the driveway at home, she saw that someone was sitting in a rocking chair on the porch.

Everett.

"What are you doing here?" Abee asked.

"It's my long weekend at home!" Everett said. "I saw that you called. I was at the airport. I figured you . . ."

Everett gave her a confused look.

"Did you forget? I don't have class tomorrow or the next day," Everett said. "Pen's on her way home too. We've been so busy getting everything done before the trip that I know we haven't talked much. But it never occurred to me that you'd forget!"

Abee laughed. Seeing Joanna, Everett hopped off the porch to come and help.

"May I . . .?" Everett started.

"Nope," Joanna said. "It's time for me to start doing for myself."

"Yes, ma'am," Everett said.

He opened the car door for Joanna and leaned over to unhook Goji. He took Abee's hand as they walked behind

Joanna toward the front door. Goji ran into the house.
Joanna came next. Everett kissed Abee's lips.

"Hi," Everett said.

"Sorry, I need a shower," Abee said.

"Yes, you do," Everett said.

Laughing, they went into the house.

NINE

Abee Normal opened her eyes to the still quiet of her great-and-then-some-grandmother's home. The predawn light filtered in through the sheer blinds of her third-floor windows. She stretched out. As her hand came down, she brushed the head of her Plott Hound, Goji the Goblin Hunter.

She sighed.

This was her favorite time of the day. She was debating rolling over and going back to sleep.

And then it started.

Again.

Like it had started every early morning.

And it would not stop until late at night.

Chatter, whisper, talking, arguing, nattering, worrying. Ugh!

This chattering hadn't stopped since the day she'd brought her mother and her grandmother back into this house.

Abee sighed and got out of bed.

She knew that she should be grateful. Her actual grandmother, Alicia Normal, was well and happy. Her mother, Joanna Normal, was still stricken with MS but was much better than she'd been just a brief time ago.

Her husband's twin, Emily, was happily settled in to her room on the second floor. She had moved in after her father hanged himself in the Beauchamps mansion. She didn't mind sharing her floor with Alicia. In fact, they'd started classes at the local community college together. The two women talked and laughed like eighteen-year-olds.

Of course, Emily *was* actually eighteen.

Abee's grandmother had just had the teenage piece of her fractured soul returned to her after Abee had freed her spirit from a sadist doctor at the Kuhn Memorial Hospital. Alicia had lived in a mental hospital all of Abee's life. Abee should not be shocked that her grandmother talked a lot. After all, she'd raised Joanna, who had more than her fair share to say.

Abee couldn't get over the sheer volume of Alicia's words.

In the presence of these women, Emily had developed the gift of gab as well.

After nearly a lifetime of living in this still, silent household, Abee was now plagued by the sound of women talking. She wouldn't mind it so much if they were talking about something.

But no.

These women woke up and started gabbing about nothing at all.

Abee couldn't sleep without earplugs. She couldn't study without her noise-canceling headphones.

And she couldn't do anything without someone listening in and commenting on it.

Her conversations with her husband, Everett Beauchamp, were monitored and then commented on.

Her conversations with her best friend, Pen Calamus, were the topic of much talk. Alicia could not get over the idea that lesbians didn't have to hide their interest in women anymore. Emily wasn't sure what it meant to be a lesbian. And Joanna vocalized whatever was on her mind.

Goji hadn't escaped their notice. Did Abee take the dog out? Did the dog get fed? Was it the right food? Was it the best food? How much was the dog eating? Had the dog gained weight?

Had Abee gained weight? Had she eaten lately? Why did she eat so much junk food? Why did she eat so much healthy food? Why did she eat so much? Why was she losing weight?

Opinions were shared, agreed upon, argued over, and shared again.

Was Abee studying too much? Maybe she was studying too little?

And what in the world was going on with Abee's hair?

She'd nearly moved out after forty-eight glorious hours in which every conversation revolved around Abee's bushy, curly, thick hair!

Abee ignored them.

Or tried to ignore them.

Today was the start of her spring break from her online college program at Hampton University. Everett was studying for finals, so she couldn't go to Princeton, where he went to school.

Pen was working on an experiment in the MIT lab and hadn't been home in days. Abee couldn't go there, either.

Abee was stuck in this house.

"Abee!" Alicia, her grandmother, yelled from under her floor boards.

Alicia was tapping the ceiling of her room with what sounded like a broom handle, making a loud "knocking" sound on the floor of Abee's room. Goji jumped up and started barking.

"Not you, too," Abee said. She pointed to the dog. "No bark!"

Goji fell silent.

"You awake?" Alicia yelled. "Joanna said you were off school this week, and I thought we could work on your hair!"

Abee swore.

"We should start before it gets too hot," Alicia said.

Abee pulled the comforter over her head.

"I bought the relaxer," Alicia yelled. "You know, the one the nurses used? The one I told you about?"

Abee sat up in bed. She threw her covers off. Like one, two, three — she went to the bathroom, changed her clothes, and ran down the stairs. She grabbed her paranormal-investigation backpack and travel bag from the front hall closet and slid out the front door, with Goji running after her.

"Took you long enough," Abee's Ma'am said.

Ma'am was sitting in a rocking chair on the porch.

"I . . ." Abee pointed back inside. She pointed to Ma'am. "You . . ."

"Where is your sprite?" Ma'am asked.

"Tippi?" Abee looked around for the five-inch fairy that followed her everywhere. "She's . . ."

Goji gave a single bark.

"Riding the dog again," Ma'am said. "Come on — we'll take my car."

"Where are we going?" Abee asked.

"Away from here," Ma'am said with a snort. "You care where?"

Abee shook her head. She was too delighted to bother asking where they were going. She dropped her supplies in the trunk of Ma'am's baby-blue 1952 Chrysler Imperial. She jogged to the back seat of the car and opened the door. Goji jumped into the back seat with Tippi on her back. Abee hopped in the passenger seat and slammed and locked the door.

"You're sure in a hurry," Ma'am said.

"I think I'm going to kill someone," Abee said softly.

"It would be justifiable homicide," Ma'am said.

Abee turned to look at Ma'am. They laughed. The Chrysler started with a resounding growl. As they drove down the driveway, they saw Alicia, Emily, and Joanna, on arm crutches, spill out of the house.

"How'd you know they had plans for me today?" Abee asked.

"It's just the kind of thing I know," Ma'am said. "You know me, I'm always trying to keep the peace."

Abee turned to look at her Ma'am. Her Ma'am was usually at the center of any controversy. She was either stirring up trouble or "fixing" some trouble she'd created or planning for the next time trouble erupted.

They drove along in silence for a moment before they both laughed again.

"Where are we going?" Abee asked.

"South Carolina," Ma'am said.

"Why?" Abee asked.

"You've been invited by the Charleston Plantation Society to clear some spirits for the nearby plantations," Ma'am said.

"How many is that?" Abee asked.

"Six," Ma'am said. "Seven, if you count the modern one. They grow tea and ghosts, apparently."

"Hrmph," Abee said. She crossed her arms over her chest. "Seven plantations? That's going to take all week."

"And then some," Ma'am said. "These are horrible places."

"Then why are we going there?" Abee asked.

"I have my reasons," Ma'am said, mildly.

"But we're getting paid, right?" Abee asked.

"You're going to have to trust me," Ma'am said.

"I thought we agreed that I would book our jobs," Abee said.

"I thought we agreed that murder was wrong," Ma'am said.

Abee gave her Ma'am a sideways look. Abee was so annoyed with the women in her life that she almost told her Ma'am to let her out.

Where would she go?

Technically, she owned the historic Beauchamps mansion and plantation. But it was in the middle of an ugly court battle. She could go stay with the Calamuses, but Jeff Calamus, Pen's father, would only put her to work clearing ghosts off of some other plantation.

She sighed.

It was either clear some plantations of some seriously nasty spirits or return to the chatterbox house to have her hair "done."

"I need to find another place to live," Abee said.

"Yep," Ma'am said.

When Ma'am responded, Abee was surprised that she'd said those words out loud.

"Let's see what we can figure out while we're on this trip," Ma'am said.

Abee nodded, more than a little relieved. She'd worried that she would offend her Ma'am by wanting to move out. But Ma'am was always on Abee's side, even when it didn't seem like it.

"You just rest for a while," Ma'am said. "It's a long drive, and you're going to have to be on your game to get through it."

"No special plane tickets from Uncle Al?" Abee asked.

"Now, if I'd told your Uncle Al that we were heading out on a trip, he'd likely tell his mother or your mother and . . ." Ma'am started.

Abee up her hands over her ears. She could hear the cacophony of chatter that would ensue. Abee glared out the window.

"I don't mind the drive," Ma'am said. "Now that you have your license, you can help out."

"I will," Abee said.

Ma'am took the on-ramp to the highway and started across the country to South Carolina. They'd been driving for about an hour when Abee turned to look at Ma'am.

"How much work do we have to do?" Abee asked.

"A lot," Ma'am said.

"Why haven't you already done it?" Abee asked.

"I wasn't invited to do it," Ma'am said. "You were invited. Abee Normal, Paranormal Investigations has a stellar reputation."

"Uh-huh," Abee said. "And what?"

"You're now one of *them*," Ma'am said.

Abee groaned and slid down in the seat.

"We are driving straight through, if that's why you're asking," Ma'am said.

Abee shook her head. Ma'am turned on her music system, and they drove along listening to Ma'am's African drum music. About three hours into the drive, Abee took over driving. The first thing she did was to take a break for food, the bathroom, and a potty break for Goji.

Sustained, Abee drove for the next eight hours. She stopped every three hours or so. With eleven hours done, they were a few hours from Charleston, South Carolina. Ma'am took over so that Abee could rest. They drove to the Plantation Inn in downtown Charleston.

"Whew," Abee said, jerking out of a sound sleep.

She stared at the hotel.

"You're not seriously thinking that we'll stay there," Abee said.

"The Plantation Society made the reservation," Ma'am said. She leaned forward to look at the hotel. "It's very nice. Expensive. Five-star rating and all of that."

"It's very haunted," Abee said. "And not in a Casper-the-Friendly-Ghost kind of way."

"Oh," Ma'am said with a sigh. "They all are."

"Every hotel in Charleston is haunted?" Abee asked. Her voice reflected her doubt.

Ma'am simply nodded. Abee looked at her Ma'am for a long moment.

"Why'd you want to come here?" Abee asked.

"I . . ." Ma'am shook her head in a way that made Abee's heart clench with pain.

"Well, I don't mind," Abee said when her Ma'am couldn't finish her sentence.

Ma'am looked relieved not to have to explain herself. She pulled up to the valet. The valet had big smiles for them. He laughed about the car and commented on Goji. Another man came to take their bags. They followed the man into the hotel. They spent only a few moments at registration before they were led up to their room. The door swung shut on a lovely two-bedroom suite, and Goji jumped onto the couch.

Ma'am took a step and started to crumple. Abee rushed to her side. She just managed to catch her before Ma'am fell to the ground. Abee negotiated Ma'am to a chair.

Ma'am mumbled something that Abee couldn't make out.

Abee knelt down in front of Ma'am and looked her in the eyes.

"You can tell me anything," Abee said.

"I . . ." Ma'am shook her head. "Evil."

Abee opened her mouth to ask why they were staying there. One glance at her Ma'am, and she knew that Ma'am lacked the stamina to move. Abee nodded.

She took out her cellphone. She poked around for a bit before dialing a number.

"Destiny?" Abee asked. "Hey, it's Abee. You know, Abee Normal from school."

"Happy break!" Destiny's bright voice was like liquid sunshine to Abee's heart.

"Remember how you said that I could come and stay in your pool house?" Abee asked.

"Of course," Destiny said. "Come for a visit! My dad's house is about twenty-five minutes from Charleston! Where are you now?"

"I'm at some hotel called the 'Plantation Inn,'" Abee said.

"Downtown," Destiny said. "I thought you ..."

"My Ma'am took a job at the local plantations," Abee said. "I didn't know about it until this morning. I was going to call to see if we could get together when we were settled, but this hotel won't work for us. We need a place to stay."

"Why?" Destiny asked. "The Plantation Inn is lovely."

Rather than explain about the ghosts and the "evil" perceived by her Ma'am, Abee simply said: "My Ma'am has taken ill. She needs some space."

"Come on over," Destiny said, her voice rising with delight. "I'm sorry that your Ma'am is ill but it will be great to meet you in person! I'll just tell my dad. We're supposed to leave for a trip to Barbados tomorrow. Do you want to come with us? I'm sure my dad won't mind."

"I have contracts with the plantations," Abee said with regret in her voice.

"To clear ghosts," Destiny said brightly.

"How did you . . .?" Abee asked.

"My dad found your website," Destiny said. "I talked so much about you after the project you did on African-American mental health. That story about your grandmother? Blew my mind. Totally. I don't think I stopped talking about it for days."

Abee didn't know what to say. She was mortified and elated at the same time.

"Can I help clear ghosts?" Destiny asked.

"I don't know," Abee said. "Right now, I need to get my Ma'am out of here."

"Say no more," Destiny said. "Come. I'll get the pool house ready. If I can help, I'd love to. Otherwise, I'll go to Barbados, and we can talk at the end of the week."

Abee's eyes welled with tears. She was always so surprised at the generosity of people.

"The work you do is important," Destiny said. "Really important. Even my Dad thinks so. So, you come here. We'll take care of you and your Ma'am so that you can send our ancestors home."

It was all Abee could do to merely nod. Her phone chimed.

"I sent the address and directions to your phone," Destiny said. "I know my dad *and* my mom are going to want to meet you. They are at work now, but I bet they'll come home just to meet you."

"Thank you," Abee said.

"Don't thank me yet!" Destiny said brightly. Her voice changed. "Do you think your Ma'am needs a doctor?"

Abee looked over to see Tippi standing on Ma'am's knee. Tippi shook her head to Abee.

"I think she just needs to get out of this place," Abee said. "You are a welcome refuge."

"Think nothing of it," Destiny said.

The line went dead. Abee picked up her backpack and cinched it onto her back. She grabbed her bag and her Ma'am's bag.

"Will you stay with Ma'am?" Abee asked Tippi.

The sprite nodded. With Goji by her side, Abee went downstairs to the valet. They waited for the car together. Abee set their belongings in the truck. Abee let Goji into the back seat and told her to stay. A fifty-dollar bill convinced the valet to let Abee leave the vehicle in front of the hotel while she went to get her Ma'am.

Abee went through the hotel and back up to the suite.

"Any change?" Abee asked Tippi.

Tippi flew to Abee's shoulder.

"Nothing," Tippi said.

"What's wrong with her?" Abee asked.

"I think she's . . ." Tippi leaned into Abee's ear and whispered in her squeaky, high-pitched voice, "bewitched."

Abee felt a shadow come near. She shivered. Without thinking, she opened her hand, and a four-inch piece of wood appeared. Abee flicked the wood,and it grew into a staff. Abee nodded and blue flame covered the staff.

"Away darkness!" Abee said.

She held the staff out to the darkness. The shadow hovered for what felt like a long moment before it disappeared.

"What was that?" Tippi asked.

"No idea," Abee said.

Abee grabbed Ma'am under the arm. She pulled Ma'am to her feet. Abee tapped the staff on the floor, and the blue flame went out. She gave the staff to Ma'am as a walking stick. Ma'am's hand naturally went around the stick. They made a slow, bone-wrenching journey down the hall, into the elevator, and out of the hotel.

Abee set Ma'am into the passenger seat of the Chrysler. She tipped the valet who told her to, "Give them hell!" Having no idea what that meant, she smiled, nodded, and ran around to the driver's seat. She punched the address into her phone, set the phone into the holder, and started the car.

They were five miles out of the city center when Ma'am took a deep breath.

"Tippi?" Abee asked.

Tippi flew over to Ma'am. Hovering in front of her face, Tippi said, "She's better but still bewitched."

Abee scowled. They drove the rest of the way in a tense silence. She turned into a wide driveway with a tall, ornate, metal gate. Abee pressed the call button. In minutes, the gate opened. Abee drove Ma'am's Chrysler Imperial up to the large house.

They were greeted at the gate by a living man. He was about fifty years old, in the uniform of a house servant. The ghost of a man in a similar outfit stood by his side. When Abee pulled up, the man went to open Ma'am's door. When the man saw who was in the seat, he backed up. His hand went to his heart. The ghost house servant fell to his knees.

By this time, Abee was out of the car. The man looked at Abee and then back at Ma'am.

"Wha . . .?" the man asked.

"She's taken ill," Abee said.

"She . . ." the man gestured to Ma'am. He dropped to his knees next to the ghost. "Ma'am?"

Ma'am's eyes moved to his face. The corners of her lips twitched upwards. The man looked at Abee and then back at Ma'am. Before Abee could say another word, the man had Ma'am out of the vehicle. Abee opened the back door to Goji.

"Stay with me," Abee said to the dog. "Heel."

Tippi flew to her shoulder.

"Sir?" Abee called ahead to the house servant.

His head flicked back in her direction, but he didn't waver from his course. He led Ma'am on a footpath that went around the large mansion. Abee and Goji followed right behind them. If the man had stopped short, they would have run over him and Ma'am. In moments, a small house next to the pool came into view. They continued down a plush, green lawn to the pool. The man opened the door to the pool house.

With more care than Abee could have imagined, the man set Ma'am into a comfortable reclining chair.

"I will bring in your baggage," he said. "May I have your keys?"

Abee gave him the car keys.

"I will move your vehicle." He nodded toward Ma'am. "Should I call the doctor?"

Intimidated by the intense man, Abee shook her head.

"Miss Destiny has been waiting for you," he said. "I am Isaiah. I am the houseman here. The spirit at my side is that of my great-grandfather, Abee Normal. He is attached to me, and I to him. Please do not break this attachment."

"I won't," Abee said.

"Thank you," Isaiah said. He and the spirit nodded in unison. "I will tell Miss Destiny that you are here. Are you up to meeting her father? Her mother?"

"What are they like?" Abee asked.

"Kind, decent people with good hearts," Isaiah said. "They were born and raised here. They know."

"They know what?" Abee asked.

"Exactly," Isaiah said.

With a nod, he and the spirit were gone. Abee blinked a few times in his direction and looked around the pool house. There was one bedroom and one bathroom. A large couch with a couple of comfortable chairs were set around a wide screen television. There was a small galley kitchen and a tiny eating area with a small table and a few chairs. Abee looked in the refrigerator, but it was empty, as were the cabinets.

She went back to Ma'am. Tippi was standing on Ma'am's thigh.

"Is she sick?" Abee asked.

"No," Tippi said. "It's more like she's in a trance."

"Have you seen this before?" Abee asked.

Tippi looked up at Abee and then back to Ma'am.

"Have you seen this before?" Abee asked again.

"I have," Tippi said. She looked back up at Abee. "I am afraid to upset Abee Normal."

"Upset me," Abee said.

"Abee's Tippi is older than Abee might think," Tippi said.

Tippi's translucent wings fluttered, and the tiny fairy batted her eyes. Abee felt a burst of air from Tippi's ridiculously long lashes fanning in her direction.

Abee was too worried to do anything other than nod.

"Tippi has seen this," the tiny fairy said. "When darker-of-skin humans were brought here on ships, they didn't want to go with the lighter-of-skin humans. The light-skin humans hired a *di'mänik*."

Abee shook her head.

"What is that? A *di'mänik*?" Abee asked, mangling the word.

"A being who is infused with darkness, possibly by possession," Tippi said. "This being practices the darkest magic."

"'Darkest magic'?" Abee asked, quickly.

"That which breaks the universal laws of nature," Tippi said with a nod. "Breaking another's will — human and fairy alike — is the darkest magic."

"Immortal?" Abee asked.

Tippi shook her head.

"Like me? Ma'am?" Abee asked.

Tippi shook her head.

"The darkness is infinite," Tippi said. "Magik a human, and that magik lasts a human lifetime. The *di'mänik* magik?"

Tippi shook her head.

"It can be eternal," Tippi said in a soft, kind voice.

"Did Ma'am know she was susceptible to this 'magic'?" Abee asked.

"I doubt it," Tippi said with a shake of her head.

"Can I break it?" Abee asked.

"I will think," Tippi said. "I will ask my kind what they know and how we can help."

Abee nodded.

"She is in no pain," Tippi added. "She is just not present."

At that moment, there was a knock on the door to the pool house. Goji gave a loud bark. Abee shushed the dog and looked at Tippi. The fairy flew to Goji's collar. Abee went to the door.

"Abee!" Destiny said.

The girl threw her arms around Abee. The girl was smaller than Abee and softer, fleshier in the way of young women. Her skin was brown in the color of expensive chocolate bars. Her hair was long and came off her head in a natural curly triangle. She smelled of berries. Abee hugged the girl tight.

"Thank you so much for saving us," Abee said.

"It's so great to meet you in person!" Destiny said. Her straight white teeth flashed in a smile. "My dad . . ."

Destiny gestured to the man standing behind her. Abee looked up at the man. He was about Abee's height. His body was fit and muscular from the gym. His skin was darker than his daughter's skin but not as dark as Abee's. He wore the pants to an expensive business suit, an expensive belt, and a pressed, button-down blue shirt. He gave Abee a strong look before holding out his hand.

"Desmond Beaune," he said.

"Abee Normal," Abee said. They shook hands. "Nice to meet you, Mr. Beaune."

"Desmond," he said. "Destiny talks about you so much that you already feel like family. Is your grandmother here?"

"Great-grandmother," Abee said. "My Ma'am is also here, but she is unwell."

Abee gestured inside.

"Thank you for providing us this refuge," Abee said. "I would be happy to pay for our lodging and food and . . ."

"You are welcome here," Desmond said. "As my guest."

"Are you sure?" Abee asked. "We're going to make a lot of money this week. It seems only fair that we pass some of that along."

"You are going to work at Beaune Hall?" Desmond asked.

Abee nodded.

"My ancestors worked those fields," Desmond said. "They lived, worked, and died there. Destiny tells me that there are records of . . ."

Desmond shook his head.

"I don't know what to believe," he said. "If you're a charlatan, I say good for you for cheating those assholes. If you're not, you're doing God's work here on earth."

Shaking her head, Abee held her hands, palms out, toward him.

"I'm just a girl — doing what I can do," Abee said. "I'm neither a God nor a charlatan."

"You are my guest," Desmond said with a nod.

"And my friend!" Destiny said.

Looking at his daughter, Desmond visibly softened.

Their lodging settled, Abee took her first look around. They were standing in a large backyard. There was an Olympic-sized pool a few feet from this pool house. There were fruit trees along the edge of the property and a space for a large vegetable garden. The house was a large, modern, two-story colonial home. Noting Abee's look, Desmond smiled.

"Would you like the tour?" Desmond asked.

"I'd love it!" Abee said. "But let me check on my great-grandmother."

She smiled at Destiny and her father before turning into the room. Ma'am hadn't moved from her seat, but her eyes seemed clearer.

"Ma'am?" Abee asked.

"Where are we?" Ma'am asked.

"My friend Destiny — you remember Destiny from school?" Abee asked.

Ma'am gave a slight nod.

"This is her house," Abee said. "They are letting us stay in their pool house."

"Destiny's father?" Ma'am asked. "I have heard his voice before."

"Desmond Beaune?" Abee asked. She gestured to the door. "He's right . . ."

Ma'am hefted herself out of the chair. Abee followed her to the door. Desmond took a step backward.

"Ma'am," Desmond said.

"Dez," Ma'am said with a smile. "I apologize. I am not feeling well."

Ma'am held her arms out. Destiny's father rushed into Ma'am's arms. They held each other for a moment while Abee and Destiny gawked.

"Dad?" Destiny asked, her voice rising.

"Destiny," Desmond said. "This is my grandfather's caregiver. She took care of him when I was a young child."

Desmond looked at Ma'am.

"You are ageless as ever," Desmond said. "Come. See my home. It will give me great pleasure to show you what I've made of myself."

"I always knew that you'd do great things," Ma'am said softly.

"You are the only one," Desmond said.

He held out his elbow. Ma'am hooked her hands around his elbow. They set off toward the house, leaving Destiny and Abee gawking at their backs. They were a few feet away when Abee noticed Tippi was riding on Ma'am's shoulder.

That was how Ma'am had the energy to talk and move around. Abee grinned at her little friend.

"I guess we should join them," Destiny said.

Abee nodded. The girls started walking toward the house.

"This makes us kind of family," Destiny said in an unsure voice. "Doesn't it?"

"It absolutely does," Abee said with a smile.

Destiny gave Abee a big grin. They started toward the house.

Destiny's mother, Nancy Jones-Beaune, came home during the house tour. She immediately cancelled their trip to Barbados and demanded to hear everything that had been said in her absence. A lawyer for the local NAACP, Nancy looked like an older version of Destiny. Her hair was naturally curly, her smile was wide, and her eyes smart and searching. After dinner, Nancy pulled Abee aside and asked if it was a bird or possibly a fairy on Ma'am's shoulder. Unwilling to lie, Abee said that Tippi was a friend. Nancy seemed to accept that at face value, but Abee knew she was going to have to explain at some point.

One thing was certain — Destiny was the much-loved only child of two power brokers.

Abee made their excuses after dinner. She led Ma'am back to the pool house. For the first time in her young life, Abee helped Ma'am get ready for bed. Abee felt like she could finally give back some of what she'd received from this amazing woman. She settled Ma'am in the bed in the bedroom and sat with her until she was sure that Ma'am was asleep.

Abee called Everett on a video call. They spoke in whispered tones so as not to disturb Ma'am. Abee went to sleep on the couch.

Abee woke before sunrise. For the first time in her life, Ma'am was still asleep when Abee awoke. She went in to wake Ma'am. She helped Ma'am through her morning routine. While Ma'am sat on the couch, Abee created the altar Ma'am usually made. When she finished, Abee lit a candle with her blue flame. She watched as Ma'am's lips moved in her morning prayers.

A knock at the door brought them breakfast. Abee hand-fed Ma'am her usual breakfast of yogurt and fruit. Ma'am drank down a strong cup of coffee. For the briefest moment, Abee thought the caffeine had revived her Ma'am. But Ma'am sighed and sank back into whatever silent terror kept her locked inside her head.

"Okay, Ma'am," Abee said. "Should I leave you here?"

Ma'am slowly shook her head. She pointed to her chest and then to Abee's chest. Abee nodded. Her Ma'am had done harder things for Abee than simply being with her when she was sick. Tippi flew onto Ma'am's shoulder to help her across the yard. Goji never left Abee's side. They made slow progress. They'd just reached Ma'am's Chrysler when Destiny came out of the house.

"We want to help," Destiny said.

She gestured behind her, where her parents were standing. The Beaune family was dressed in jeans and T-shirts. They were ready for work in the field.

Unsure of what to do and not knowing how to stop them, Abee acquiesced.

"Just follow me," Abee said.

Destiny gave a cheer.

"We go to Beaune first," Abee said.

"We're right behind you," Desmond said.

As the family stepped out of the door, Tiana, the cook, and Isaiah followed behind. Everyone in this house wanted to help Abee.

Sure she was going to regret this, Abee started Ma'am's car and drove to Beaune Hall. She had a quick conversation with the owners before being introduced to the plantation's manager, Gordon Johnson. She followed the plantation manager to the fields they were concerned about. He was a tall, thin man with short-cropped grey hair, milk-chocolate skin, and blue-grey eyes. His extensive lines and wrinkles were a testament to his having spent a lifetime outdoors.

"This is them," Gordon Johnson said. "They were just cleared of early crop."

He looked toward the field, but his dark eyes flicked back to Abee. He watched her looking out across the fields. Abee saw a few hundred human spirits stooped over crops that they were harvesting or sowing. Some of them were weeding. A few were hand-watering each plant from buckets. More than a few young female spirits had babies tied to their backs.

"I see," Abee said. "Thank you for showing me, Mr. Johnson."

"Call me Gord," he said.

"Sir," Abee said.

He leaned in her direction.

"Can you see 'em?" he asked.

Abee turned toward him. She gave him a long, assessing look.

"What?" he asked. "D'ju hex me?"

"Not yet," Abee said with a grin.

Shocked, he jerked himself to look at her. Seeing her grin, he laughed with relief.

"I was trying to assess what you'd like me to say," Abee said.

He sucked in a slow breath through his teeth while he thought it through.

"You done a lot of these?" he asked.

"I've done a bit," Abee said. "Where we live. That's how the owners heard about me and my Ma'am. You can imagine that there are a lot of fields like this in America. Some have been built on. Many are sitting fallow. There's a lot of work to be done."

Abee looked at the man for a moment before adding, "How are we to move forward if we don't let these souls have their rest? They anchor us in the horrible past."

Gordon's eyes flicked to her again. He grunted and then bent over to look at Ma'am through the passenger window. He caught a look at Goji in the back seat.

"Okay," he said with nod. "I want to know."

"About?" Abee asked.

"I want to know if you can see them," he said. "I want to know why they are stuck here. I want to ..."

He shook his head. He took a blue ball cap out of his back pocket and jammed it on his head. The bill shaded his eyes from the brightening day.

"I can see them," Abee said. "They are working the fields. Planting or harvesting — both. Tending plants. Some are weeding or watering. Depends on the field."

"Why ...?" he asked.

"Why are they stuck?" Abee asked. Her cheeks puffed out as she let out a slow breath. "I can only give you my opinion, which is based on my rather limited experience."

"You got more than me," he said. "You go ahead."

"We talk about the ships that brought Africans to this continent. The Middle Passage. The slave-ship owners," Abee said. "We rarely talk about — and simply cannot understand — what happened to get these souls to the slavers."

He gave a little nod.

"So, to answer your question, it's been my experience that they don't know where to go," Abee said. "Even if they were in Africa, there are those who could not go home. Some of them were kidnapped. A few were betrayed by friends or family. More than a few were sold to slavers. None of them are exactly certain where they are in the world. They know for absolute certain that they cannot walk or swim home from here."

Gordon's face pinched, as if he was experiencing her words firsthand. Abee continued.

"This experience was so jarring that it disrupted their spiritual connection to their spiritual home," Abee continued. "Having their freedom taken from them and everything else that went along with slavery only made it worse."

"So they keep working," he said under his breath.

"Again, that's just my experience and my opinion," Abee said. She turned and grinned at him. "I haven't met your ghosts yet. Maybe they're here for the food."

He grinned at her.

"Can I help?" he asked.

"I'm not sure how," Abee said. She gestured to the vehicle behind Ma'am's Chrysler. "My friend from college is here with her parents. They want to help, too. I've never had anyone besides my Ma'am help, so I don't really know what that would look like."

Gordon gave her a bright smile.

"I'll tell our cook," he said. "You'll have good food."

"Sounds great," Abee said.

She held out her hand, and he shook it. She went back to Ma'am's Chrysler and drove to a shady spot. She set Ma'am's folding chair under a tree near the field and helped her Ma'am there. She went back to the car to get her gear. When she returned, there was a large thermal container with water in it and paper cups. Destiny, her parents, Tiana, and Isaiah were setting up under the same tree.

"What can we do?" Destiny's mother, Nancy, asked.

"I am not sure," Abee said. "I need to go out there and see what I can learn. There may be a specific-to-this-place reason these souls are trapped here. I won't know until I ask."

Nancy and Desmond gave Abee a firm nod. Destiny looked disappointed.

"I'll let you know when I figure out what you can do!" Abee said brightly.

She needed to find something for them to do. Otherwise, they would be driving her crazy in no time.

She put her hand on her chest. Her blue flame protective layer appeared. She touched Goji, and the dog was covered with the same blue flame. After Tippi's capture and torture at the hands of a rival sprite kingdom, Tippi had insisted on being protected by the blue flame. Abee gave it to her. Tippi was also given a spear by the weapons master of her people. She'd been taking lessons. She stood on Abee's shoulder with her suit of blue fire and her sharp fairy spear.

Abee opened her hand, and a four-inch piece of wood appeared. She shook out her hand. The wood grew into a staff. Abee nodded, and the wooden staff was covered in blue flame. She turned and pointed the end of the staff at her great-etc. grandmother. The blue flame covered and protected her Ma'am.

Abee looked at the Beaunes. Like most humans, they could not see the blue flame.

Abee, Goji, and Tippi started out into the field. In the spirit dimension, they shone like beacons.

Yet, no spirit looked up at her. It was as if she didn't exist.

She tried the trick where she created a vortex to pull the souls from the field. It rarely worked in these fields, but it was always worth a try.

It didn't work at all.

Even with the vortex, no soul bothered to even look up. She'd never seen anything like this. It was as if they were in a trance, like Ma'am. Sighing, she went back to sit with Ma'am under the tree to think. Nancy passed Abee a cold soda from their cooler.

"Can we help?" Destiny asked again.

"I need to think," Abee said. "If my Ma'am wasn't ill, she'd know what to do."

"She always did," Desmond said with a snort.

His response made Abee smile. She hadn't realized that she'd been so worried about Ma'am. Abee reached over to hold Ma'am's hand.

Tippi poked Abee with the end of her spear.

"Look," Tippi said.

Tippi pointed out into the field. There, in the middle of the field, stood a flimsy, see-through projection of Abee's Ma'am. It flashed with blue light and then went out, only to brighten again.

"Ma'am," Abee said under her breath.

Ma'am began a series of gestures. It took Abee a moment before she realized that Ma'am was using American Sign Language to communicate with Abee. Her mind flushed with the warmth of memory.

Prior to Abee living with Ma'am, Abee hadn't had anyone telling her what or how to do things. Her mother was ill with multiple sclerosis. Abee had raised herself.

But Ma'am's house had rules.

And Ma'am was willing to do whatever it took to get Abee to follow them.

So, Abee stopped talking.

Period. She wouldn't talk at school, and she certainly wouldn't talk at home. After a week of that, Ma'am started signing to her. Furious, Abee had flung herself from the house. When she'd returned, she'd found a book on American Sign Language — "ASL" — on her bed. For the next few months, she and Ma'am communicated only with sign language.

Abee smiled at the warmth of the memory. Once again, Ma'am was doing whatever it took to reach Abee when Abee needed her.

"Plant. S . . . A . . . G . . . E . . ." Abee said under her breath. "Humans."

Abee blinked rapidly as she thought it through.

"Really?" Abee asked in ASL.

Ma'am's head went up and down in an exaggerated nod.

"How do I free you?" Abee's heart broke in helpless longing.

Ma'am shook her head and signed, "Dangerous."

Abee knew that she could never talk her Ma'am into doing something that was dangerous to Abee. She wondered what this projection had cost her Ma'am.

Ma'am spelled out, "Blue flame."

"Oh?" Abee asked in ASL. "You can do this because of the protection of the flame?"

Ma'am gave an exaggerated nod.

"Good to know," Abee said.

"Get to work," Ma'am signed. "Stop lazing about!"

Grinning at the projection, Abee squeezed her Ma'am's hand and let it go. She went to the trunk of the car where they always kept the bundled dried white sage they had harvested from the field of white sage planted behind Ma'am's house. She'd just reached for the box of sticks made from the Palo Santo trees in Ma'am's forest when she heard a car door slam. Closing the trunk, she looked up.

Destiny and her parents were not the only humans watching and waiting for Abee.

Twenty-three people — male and female of all races – were now standing by the side of the road. As she watched, a squadron of green golf carts, led by the plantation manager, Gordon Johnson, drove down the road in her direction.

"Quite a crowd," Abee said.

"I'm so sorry," Destiny said. "It's my fault. I put out on Instagram that we were here to clear out some ghosts, and people started showing up. I had no idea."

"I wouldn't have believed it," Abee said.

"I guess we all want our ancestors to be at peace," Nancy, Destiny's mother, said.

Abee nodded.

"I came up with a way you can help," Abee said. "These spirits are in a kind of trance. Like my Ma'am. They need to be awakened before they can be released from this field."

Abee nodded.

"What can we do?" Nancy asked.

"I'd like you to walk through the fields while burning this sage or the Palo Santo sticks," Abee said. "They are both powerful cleansers of negative energy. One might work better than the other in this situation. We have to try it. Hopefully, they will break the spell long enough for me to release the spirits."

"Got it," Nancy said.

She and her husband, Desmond, shared a long look before he nodded. He stepped forward to speak to those who had arrived. As Gordon passed Destiny's father, he shook his hand and said a few words.

"What does your father do?" Abee asked.

"Oh," Destiny sighed. "He used to own an Internet company, but he sold it."

"Then how...?" Abee asked, nodding to where Gordon and Desmond were talking.

"He's running for mayor," Destiny said. "That's why I'm in online school. You know, show family unity and all?"

Abee gave Destiny a questioning look, and the girl shrugged. Gordon came to talk to Abee.

"Have you started?" the plantation manager asked.

"Just about to," Abee said.

"We had a meeting and decided that this field clearing was the most important thing we could do today," Gordon said with a nod of his head. "How can we help?"

"Do you have any white sage bundles?" Abee asked.

"We sure don't," Gordon said. "They sell what we grow in the gift shop. They go right away, so I'd be surprised if there were any left from the fall."

"I have it," Abee said. "Palo Santo, too."

"Did you say 'Palo Santo'? *Bursera graveolens*?" Gordon asked.

"Yes," Abee said.

"We have an entire field of it," Gordon said. "They were planted in the 1800s in a dry field near the edge of the plantation. It grows like weeds. If I don't cut it back, it will take over the entire place. There was a lot of damage from that big storm last year. It took us a month to clear it up."

"Oh?" Abee asked, wondering what he was telling her.

"Let's just say that I have a lot of it," Gordon said.

"I use it in these sticks," Abee said. She opened her hand to show five-inch-long, one-inch-wide slivers of wood. "But anything will work."

"I'm on it," Gordon said.

Gordon whistled to his team, and they walked toward him. He spoke to them briefly. Two men went to their carts and drove off in the same direction. A woman started off in her cart in another direction.

Abee was about to tell people what she wanted to do when she heard Destiny talking.

"Now, don't overwhelm her," Destiny said. "She has important work to do."

"I am unclear on what we are to do," a light-skinned woman with a heavy southern accent said.

Abee stepped forward, and everyone looked at her. She put her hand on Destiny's shoulder.

"These souls seem to be in a kind of trance," Abee said. "We're going to burn some white sage and some Palo Santo..."

"The holy tree," a voice came from the back.

"Exactly," Abee said. "I believe that the smoke will break the trance for a moment. Once the trance is broken, I'll send them on home."

There was a general positive murmur in the crowd.

"Some advice," Abee said. "Leave your phones and other electronics in the car. Heavy spirit activity can mess with the electronics. I have ruined my phones this way. Watches and key fobs, too."

Everyone stared at Abee.

"There is often a kind of wind or fog when the spirits start to leave," Abee said. "If you have a bandanna or a handkerchief..."

"A towel?" someone on the side asked.

"Anything to cover your mouth so you don't get too much dust," Abee said. "If you help, expect to need a shower afterwards."

"Will the spirits hurt us?" a tan-skinned young woman with a squeaky voice asked.

"As a general rule, no," Abee said. "I should be able to protect you. If something does happen, I can assist you in returning to whole."

"That doesn't sound good," someone said.

Abee shrugged and started passing out the sage and Palo Santo sticks. Destiny walked behind her, lighting the sage and Palo Santo. Destiny arranged everyone in a line across the length of the field. When the smoke from the sage and the Palo Santo billowed, they walked one step at a time across the field.

Abee walked behind them.

The smoke hit the first spirits and . . .

Nothing happened.

Abee wanted to cry. Then she remembered that most spirits need reminding that they are free and can go. Abee touched the soul of a young woman on her shoulder.

"You are free," Abee said.

The young woman looked up at Abee. For a moment, the woman looked at her without seeing. And then, a dawning realization came over the soul.

"You are free," Abee repeated.

The woman's face brightened. She stood up and said something in another language. The souls near her looked up at her. The woman lifted her eyes to the sky.

In a moment, she was gone.

One by one, the souls around her looked toward the heavens and disappeared. Mothers grabbed their children and danced away. Ahead of the smoke, spirits continued to work, but behind them, the spirits drifted home.

Abee grinned at the sound of the celebration starting on the other side.

Abee heard something — not a sound, really, but a kind of movement in the energetic field that made a sort of "ping." Abee looked around to see what was making that sound.

Directly behind her stood Tlanuwa, the Mother of the Sacred Flame's Native American priest.

Abee and Ma'am had met him when they'd resolved an energetic vortex from the Emerald Mound. The Mother of the Sacred Flame had assisted in Abee's transformation from confused human teenager to confused whatever-she-was-now. The Mother had endued Abee with the blue sacred flame. Abee had not seen the priest since he left this realm to serve the Mother of the Sacred Flame.

She turned around to look at him. Goji barked in recognition. The priest was intently watching the activity on the field. When he didn't gesture her to him, she turned back to the work of releasing souls. She walked the entire field as she searched for other souls. She continued working to release souls until the humans waited on the other side of the field. Reaching the other side of the field, she beamed at the people who had helped.

"Is it done?" Nancy, Destiny's mother, asked.

"They have gone home," Abee said.

They gave a loud cheer. People seemed genuinely happy. Abee laughed.

When she turned back, the priest was gone. She felt a knot of worry begin in her belly.

"Where to next?" Destiny asked, her face bright with accomplishment.

"We have six more fields," Abee said. "We can..."

She looked up to see Gordon. The woman he'd sent off in her golf cart was standing right behind him.

"We lost a lot of branches in that hurricane," Gordon said. "I thought maybe, instead of those little sticks, you could burn these?"

"Great idea," Abee said.

"I sent the other two to start bonfires with this wood in the other fields," Gordon said.

"That's fantastic!" Abee said.

Destiny waved the people back to their cars. Abee found Ma'am standing with Destiny's father. Ma'am's face was blank, but at least she was standing. Desmond congratulated Abee and shook her hand. He helped her get Ma'am back into the vehicle. Abee went to quickly pack their gear. She opened the door for Goji. The dog jumped into the back seat. Abee took the driver's seat.

"Did you see that priest?" Tippi asked in her high, mouse-like voice

The fairy climbed up onto the dashboard. Abee started the car and began to follow Gordon to the group of fields about a mile from the house.

"I did," Abee said. "He didn't say anything."

"He looked worried," Tippi said.

"There's a lot of moving parts in these expeditions," Abee said.

"About you," Tippi said. "He seemed worried about *you*."

"I wonder why," Abee said. "Did you see the Mother?"

"No, no," Tippi said. "I did not. The fact that he's here is bad. If she showed up . . ."

Tippi shook her head again.

"Bad?" Abee asked.

"I've never seen the Mother," Tippi said. "And I am grateful for that. It's said that she shows up only when serious evil is afoot."

"Locking those souls to the field is evil," Abee said. "What's happening with my Ma'am is evil."

Tippi nodded.

"Whatever it is — it is worse than that," Tippi said.

"Something to look forward to," Abee said under her breath.

She pulled the vehicle over to the side of the road. Empty fields went at least a mile off the left-hand side of the field.

"Maybe he's here to help," Abee said what she knew wasn't true.

"Sure," Tippi said mildly.

Shaking her head, Abee got out of the vehicle. The people who had helped followed Abee to the new fields.

Abee went to the edge of the field to take a look.

The field consisted of nearly 160 acres of continuous growing space. Abee looked across the field and let out a slow whistle. There were a lot of souls here.

She had heard about slavery all of her life. They had studied it in school. She'd read a lot of books and had grown up around Ma'am's friends. She thought that she knew and understood slavery.

But standing here, on the edge of this field, she could see with her own eyes the sheer human cost. Abee sighed.

There was nothing she could do about what had happened in the past.

But she could help these souls find peace.

When she turned back to the car, she saw Ma'am. She said a silent prayer that she would be able to help her Ma'am.

She waved to Gordon, and he jogged over to her.

"Bonfires?" Abee asked.

"Should we light them up?" Gordon asked.

He gave her a big smile. She felt a stab of insecurity.

"It might not work," Abee said.

Gordon gave a stiff nod. Abee sighed.

"Light them up," Abee said.

Gordon gave her a broad grin. He whistled to his men. Grinning, they waved back. They took lighters from their pocket and lit torches. A cheer went up among the people watching, and Abee looked.

There were more than fifty people here and more coming.

She swallowed hard. The bonfires burst into bright yellow flame. She was about to say something when another employee ran to the bonfire with fresh leaves. The bonfire began to smoke. One at a time, the bonfires came to light and shifted to thick smoke.

Abee watched the souls.

No one stopped their labor. They were still in a trance.

"Destiny!" Abee yelled for her friend.

Destiny and her parents ran over to Abee.

"Can you get people to stand on the fields?" Abee asked. "I know they are big, but we need humans, too."

"Could they just stand on the side?" Gordon asked. "Summer crops are to be planted this week. Some of this land is rented to sharecroppers. They can't afford to have anyone mess with the soil."

"Let's try it," Abee said with a nod.

Destiny nodded. She and her parents ran to tell people to stand on the outside of the fields. Abee went to the car to get her Ma'am and Goji. People were milling around the fields, so Abee found a quiet spot under some old trees on the other side of the road.

She looked up to see souls hanging in the trees.

"These souls aren't bewitched, Abee Normal." A male sprite came out from under a branch.

He was garbed in the ornate dress of an official of the sprite court. As was the way of sprites, he did not introduce himself.

Seeing the sprite, Tippi threw herself into the bottom of Abee's pocket. Abee could feel Tippi vibrate with fear in her pocket.

"Tippi is here as my friend and guide," Abee said to the sprite. "She means you no harm and hopes that she has not violated your customs or the sacred boundaries of your kingdom."

Sprites have a complicated system of royalty, in which every sprite is precious, but any sprite outside of their home kingdom is considered a threat.

"We are well aware of Abee Normal, Goji, and her Tippi," the male sprite said. "We are grateful if you would release the poor souls in our woods."

"Consider it done," Abee said.

Abee opened her staff. She took a moment to protect herself, Goji, Tippi, and finally Ma'am. With a flick of her wrist, she sent these souls to their spiritual home. They were drifting away when she felt Goji stiffen at her side.

A deep rumble came from Goji's chest.

A young male soul was leaning down to Ma'am. He looked to be about Abee's age, maybe a few years older. His face was inches in front of Ma'am's. He was speaking softly in some language that Abee didn't understand.

"Who are you?" Abee asked. "Tell me now, or I will send you somewhere you do not wish to be."

The male soul turned to look at Abee. While he took in every inch of her, she looked him over. He was thickly muscled and nearly as tall as Abee. For the time he came from, he would have been enormous. He wore brown pants but no top. His back was a crosshatch of thin lines made by scars.

"Who is this to you?" the male soul asked, gesturing to Ma'am.

"Who is she to you, spirit?" Abee asked, her irritation rising. "I've got too much to do to fool around with the likes of you."

She drew back with the staff.

"She is my mother," the male soul said.

Abee's mouth dropped open. She had not expected him to say anything like this. She simply blinked at him. Goji grumbled again.

"I am Abraham," the male soul said. "This is the woman who gave birth to me. She raised me until I was ten years old. Taught me to read and write. She believed . . ."

His emotions rose. Matching her irritation, he gave a brusque nod to Ma'am.

"Who is she to you?" Abraham asked.

"I'm Abee. Abee Normal. She is my kin and my friend," Abee said. "I will protect her."

"You did a great job here," Abraham said in mild rebuke.

"I didn't know that she needed protecting," Abee said. She leaned on her spear. "And anyway, *she* is the one who set up this trip."

"What year is it?" Abraham asked.

"2019," Abee said.

Abraham nodded.

"And that means?" Abee asked.

Abraham jerked to look at Abee. Her words had made him angry. The emotion flashed over his face. Seeing her sincerity, he softened.

"She didn't tell you," Abraham said.

"She told me that she had her reasons for coming here," Abee said. "I don't pry into the business of people I respect."

"Maybe you should," Abraham said.

"Listen," Abee said. "I have an entire field of souls to send home. After this field, I've got six more plantations to clear. Ma'am usually helps me, but she's sick so I . . ."

"Why do you suppose these souls are stuck here?" Abraham asked.

"I'm not sure," Abee said. "I've worked on other plantations. There are usually some souls still working — those who can't go home or have lost their way or are simply caught in their trauma. There are so many souls here. I've never seen anything like it."

Abraham dropped down into a crouch. His hands went over Ma'am's hands.

"I wish I could feel her skin," Abraham said. "She had the best skin."

After a moment, he stood up.

"If you are my mother's kin, then you are my kin," Abraham said. "Tell me, daughter, are you enslaved?"

"Me?" Abee asked. "No."

"How many are enslaved in 2019?" Abraham asked.

"Enslaved?" Abee asked. She shook her head. "None."

Surprised, Abraham's hand went to his heart, and stepped backwards.

"I mean, there are some," Abee said. "In the world. In the country. But it's illegal, and there are groups at the FBI who track the slave-traders down — we call them 'human traffickers' now —and make those jerks go to prison for a long time."

Abee stopped talking.

"You have no idea what I'm talking about," Abee said.

"I can't believe that there are no slaves," he said. "How do they work the fields?"

"Big machines," Abee said. "Immigrants. They don't pay them much, but they aren't enslaved."

Abraham's head went up and down in a slow nod.

"I never believed her," Abraham said. He dropped down to Ma'am again. "I am so sorry, Ma'am. I should have believed."

"She told you that slavery wouldn't last?" Abee asked.

"She told all of us," Abraham said. "We didn't dare to believe her. She said that one day there would be schools and colleges. She said one day we'd live free — to work where we wanted, to do what we wanted, to live anywhere we wanted, and even to make our money where we wanted. Is that true?"

"Basically," Abee said.

He gave a delirious laugh. His head went back, and he jumped for joy. He "hooted" a few times before doing a weird little dance. He went to Abee and tried to pick her up.

And then he stopped.

"I am dead," he said.

For the briefest moment, he looked truly sad before his face broke open in a smile.

"You are my kin," Abraham said. "I am your ancestor, and *you,* my daughter, get to live in those times."

"My mother and her mother as well," Abee said.

"That's enough for me," Abraham said. "Daughter, you are enough."

He leaned over to kiss Ma'am's face.

"I am sorry that I didn't believe," he said.

Before Abee could recover, he turned to go.

"Wait!" Abee demanded.

Abraham turned to look at her.

"What has a hold of my Ma'am?" Abee asked.

He gave her a long look before stepping forward, toward her. He stood less than an inch from her.

"There was a man," Abraham said. "He would tie up the will of a person so that they didn't fuss over what was done to them."

"How do I . . .?" Abee started.

"You'll see him soon enough," Abraham said. He nodded to the bon fires. "That fire from the 'holy stick' trees."

"Palo Santo," Abee said.

"I was there when those trees were planted on my mother's instruction," he said. "It was to break his hold over us. It must have worked."

"It's working now," Abee said.

"That grove still here?" Abraham asked.

"It was damaged by a big hurricane, but it's still standing," Abee nodded.

"Of course, it is," Abraham said.

"How do I defeat him?" Abee asked.

"I doubt you can," Abraham said.

"My Ma'am must have," Abee said. "I mean, until now."

"No," Abraham said. "She was too dangerous to keep here. They sold her on. She told him that she needed to be free to leave. He agreed to free her but only if she returned on a specific interval. 16 years, I believe."

Abraham nodded to Ma'am.

"She's returned on the interval," Abraham said.

"Why would she do that?" Abee asked, horrified by what he was saying.

"Now, that question is not mine to answer," Abraham said.

They fell silent. The ghost appeared to be waiting for Abee to ask the right question

"Surely, he's not still living," Abee said.

"Doesn't matter," Abraham said. "Not one bit."

He nodded his head to the field.

"They don't seem to notice," Abraham said.

He looked at Abee.

"My last wish is fulfilled," Abraham said.

"I can send you home," Abee said.

"Daughter, I believe you need me here to help you," Abraham said.

"How can you help me?" Abee asked.

"I will lead you to him," Abraham said.

"What is his name?" Abee asked.

"He used to go by the name 'Cofachiqui,'" Abraham said.

"Like the tribe?" Abee asked. "Were they from here?"

"He is not a native," Abraham said. "He thought the name made him seem more mystical. He wore loin cloths and native headdresses. His skin was brown, but he was Spanish. From Barbados."

Destiny called to Abee. Abee turned and waved.

"That's a lot of living humans," Abraham said.

"They're here to help set their ancestors free," Abee said.

"There're white people there," Abraham said.

"White people are stuck, as well," Abee said. "Their ancestors are either on that field or responsible for someone else being on a field. They want to heal the past. It's . . . important."

"I see." Abraham gave a long, disbelieving nod.

"We were talking about a guy? Sorcerer?" Abee asked.

"He was chased from of Barbados for sorcery," Abraham said. "But he set up shop here. Made a fortune."

"He's dead, right?" Abee asked.

"Evil magic does not die when the body gives out," Abraham said.

"What is his name?" Abee asked.

"He will hear me the moment I say his name," Abraham said. "I will stay with you until you need to confront him."

"There is so much to do," Abee said with a sigh as she looked out over the fields of still-working ghosts. "We'll have to start tomorrow morning."

"Night time is the best time to confront evil," Abraham said.

"Really?" Abee asked.

"Yes, daughter," Abraham said. "Human's lose power in the dark. Even evil created by *dí'mänik* inside a human is still human evil. Human evil is lessened by the lack of light."

Wondering if he was right, Abee gave him a vague nod.

"Finish up with these fields, and we'll go hunting," Abraham said.

"You'll tell me his name then?" Abee asked. "I can't destroy him without his name."

"Of course," Abraham said.

"I need to . . ." Abee said.

"Go on, daughter," Abraham said. "Release the souls of our people. I will wait with my mother."

Abee nodded. With Goji at her side and Tippi hiding in her pocket, Abee started across the road to the field. She'd almost reached the other side when two local news vans pulled up right in front of her. Abee groaned.

Ma'am's little trip to Charleston had become news.

Shaking her head at the news vans, Abee moved her right hand in an arch to give her relative invisibility. Ma'am had taught her the technique when she was young. The idea was that, when people looked at her, they had the desire to look away. Ma'am had said that it was regularly used by slaves so that they didn't attract attention from the planters. Abee hoped it worked for newspeople as well.

"Abee!" Destiny said. "Everyone's lined up on the edges!"

"Did you pass out the sage?" Abee asked.

Destiny nodded.

"People brought their own," Destiny said. "I guess someone tweeted that they needed sage. A local spiritualist store is donating these small sage bundles."

Destiny put one in Abee's hand. Abee looked it over and then put it to her nose. She pulled a breath through her nose and smelled — sunshine, healthy soil, clean water, and well-intentioned people making these bundles. Nodding, Abee gave the bundle back to Destiny.

"They should work," Abee said.

She looked out onto the field. The Palo Santo bonfires filled the air with billowing grey smoke. She glanced over at the news crew to see Destiny's father talking to them. She looked back at Destiny.

"They saw the smoke," Destiny said in answer to Abee's unspoken question.

Abee nodded.

"I'm going to head out," Abee said. "Can you remind people about their phones? A field this large, their phones and exercise watches, things like that, will likely short out or worse."

"Worse?" Destiny asked.

"Pick up a spirit," Abee said.

"Really?" Destiny asked.

"I've seen it before," Abee said, lifting an eyebrow.

Destiny nodded sincerely. She walked over to her mother, who appeared to be in full organizing mode. Freeing ghosts usually didn't look like much. If she wanted to keep doing this work, she needed a whirl of activity to distract the television news. In order to give people time to put their possessions away, Abee began to slowly walk past the souls working in the spirit field. Goji stayed rooted to her side. Halfway through their walk, Tippi came out of Abee's pocket to stand on her shoulder.

She walked about a half mile to where she judged was near the center of the 160-acre field. There was a near-deafening cacophony of spirit activity here as men and women bent over long-dead cotton or tobacco plants.

Abee tried to pick a spot to stand where the spirits were not working. From where she stood, she could see individual time frames from as early as the 1850s through the Civil War and even until current times. She'd never seen anything like it. On this field, the past and the present seemed to exist at the same moment.

Each soul's sole focus was his or her work. An inch from where she stood, a deep-dark-skinned man, naked from the waist up, was whacking at the soil with a hoe. His glistening skin dropped moisture where a lighter-skinned woman from a different era bent to pick cotton from a plant. A ten-year-old barefoot child with a round face from still another time was watering a long-gone plant with a bucket.

Abee wished that Ma'am was here to explain what was going on.

Sighing to herself, Abee looked up to see the people lining the field lighting their sage bundles.

She heard someone yelling. She glanced around to see that a woman had moved out onto the field. From where Abee stood, she could see that the woman was standing on top of a spirit, who was obliviously picking what looked to Abee like cucumbers. Abee scowled.

The woman was screaming about the horrible suffering that she felt went on in this field.

"News of the obvious," Abee said under her breath.

She had no idea why anyone would pretend that they interacted with the spirit realm and didn't bother to help trapped spirits. The spiritualist woman reached a hand out to Abee.

"She ... she ..." the woman yelled.

Irritated, Abee opened her hand, and another staff appeared. She tapped it to the ground. Immediately, a cyclone-like whirlwind began to circle the outer edges of the field. Abee was now hidden behind this dust storm.

The spiritualist woman squealed as dirt and dust battered her. Someone pulled her off the field.

Shaking her head, Abee was about to opening the heavens when she saw the Mother of the Sacred Flame's priest walking purposefully toward her. Abee raised her hand overhead to wave at him. With her invitation, Tlanuwa hopped to where she stood.

"Tlanuwa." She gave Tlanuwa an awkward bow.

"Abee Normal." With much greater ease, Tlanuwa bowed to her.

"What brings you here?" Abee asked.

"The Mother sent me," Tlanuwa said. "This creature you are dealing with will not be easily destroyed."

"This creature?" Abee asked.

"You did not think that such malevolence could be human, did you?" Tlanuwa asked.

"Yes," Abee said. She gestured around her. "It doesn't take much for me to believe that humans can be evil."

Tlanuwa gave her a slight smile.

"Your presence will be immediately noticed the moment you relieve him of these souls," Tlanuwa said.

"Any tips on staying under his radar?" Abee asked.

"There is no way," Tlanuwa said.

"Then how do you recommend?" Abee asked. "I mean, all of these people are here to see me do this thing and

. . . These souls deserve to be free, to go home to see their families again, to be at peace."

Tlanuwa nodded.

"You know this more than anyone else," Abee said.

"I do," Tlanuwa said.

"What do I do?" Abee asked.

Tlanuwa pointed to the woman picking cotton, to the man hitting the field with his hoe, and finally to the child watering a different plant.

"What do you see here?" Tlanuwa asked.

"I've never seen anything like it. Weird, isn't it?" Abee asked. "What do you think it is?"

"You are looking into time itself," Tlanuwa said. "All three souls worked on this tiny bit of land."

"I'm looking in . . ." Abee said. "What does that mean?"

"Time is not linear," Tlanuwa said.

"I've heard that," Abee said.

"In our way of thinking," Tlanuwa said, "time is like a ribbon. It folds onto itself, wraps around, and sticks together in places."

"Okay," Abee said.

Not sure what to say to the ancient priest, Abee nodded.

"You are looking at a place where the ribbon of time is folded onto itself," Tlanuwa said. "Notice how each of these souls crosses one section of the earth. This is where they are pinned to this ribbon of time. The man who held these souls here had locked only one of them into this fold of time. However, as time continued, any soul that engaged this spot and was under his influence was trapped here."

"How do I unlock it?" Abee asked. "Free them?"

"You must hunt him," Tlanuwa said. "Destroy the creature that has taken hold of his soul. Release his greedy soul, or destroy it."

"We can destroy a soul?" Abee asked.

"Some souls cannot be healed or fixed," Tlanuwa said. "They must return to dust and be reforged."

"Good to know," Abee said. "You know, I can't really just leave here."

Abee gestured to the field around her.

"You are standing near a pin in the ribbon of time," Tlanuwa said. "From this point, the Sacred Flame can take you wherever you wish to go. You know that."

"Tippi, hold on," Abee said. "Goji?"

Abee leaned down to grab her dog's collar. Tlanuwa took her arm. Abee flicked the staff, and it became covered with blue flame. She protected Goji and Tippi.

"Do you need . . .?" Abee asked Tlanuwa.

"I am a part of the Sacred Flame now," Tlanuwa said. "I am she, and she is me. This is how I can appear before you in this time."

"Okay," Abee said. "Here we go."

Abee stepped onto the spot where Tlanuwa said the ribbon of time was pinned.

"I wish to see . . ." Abee said and stopped talking. She had no idea who to ask for. For lack of anything else, she said, "The maker of this pin."

Like some cheesy 1970s television show, the world seemed to spin. Abee was just about to say something about reruns when Tlanuwa spoke.

"We are spinning on the pin," Tlanuwa said. "Ask for the beginning, for the originator."

Abee grinned at him. She tapped her staff on the point and demanded to be taken to beginning of this stuck point and its originator.

Abee had expected to feel as if they were riding a water slide or maybe a roller coaster, flying along the ribbon of time. What happened was much weirder.

Abee took a breath and made her request.

They were standing in what looked like a cobbler's shop before Abee had fully exhaled.

The walls of the shop were lined with shoes — some made of delicate lace and silk, while others looked like they could withstand years of hard labor. The air smelled like leather and some kind of tallow. The small, dark shop was lit with oil lamps along the walls. There was a noisy clock ticking on the wall.

They were standing behind two men. One man was hunched over the table, working on a pair of dress boots. The other was standing beside the first. They were arguing in fierce, quiet language. Their body odor rose off them in waves.

"You should not have come," the man at the table said. "You're going to get me killed."

"I will protect you," the other man said. "No one can break my spells."

"Spells! Magic!" the cobbler said. "Where did that get you in Barbados?"

For a moment, Abee wondered why she was able to understand these men. Tlanuwa pointed to the blue flame that covered her ears. The flame was translating what they were saying into English.

"I made a lot of money," the second man said.

"You were chased out of the country!" the cobbler said. "If anyone finds out you're here, you are to be returned to Barbados."

The cobbler turned in his chair to look at the other man.

"There's a noose waiting for you in Barbados," the cobbler said. His finger poked the man in the chest. "Don't you dare bring your evil into my city. I won't protect you from what comes."

The cobbler pointed to the ground.

"This city will not stand for your dark magic," the cobbler said.

"We'll see about that," the second man said. "It's 1856. I was invited here to work for Mr. Ryan at his new Auction Mart."

"At least a million slaves have been sold out in the open markets and wharves of Charleston," the cobbler said derisively. "Why would Councilman Ryan need you?"

"They need to be submissive to be sold inside the building," the second man said. "I've got just the thing to make them do what they are told."

"With witchcraft," the cobbler said.

"Witchcraft?" the second man sniffed. "The *dí'mänik* power fills me now. There is no beginning of me that doesn't end in the power of magic."

Abee grabbed Goji's collar and gave it a quick tug. The dog looked up at her. Abee gave her the signal to "mark it." Goji's eyes looked at the cobbler. Abee shook her head. Goji looked at the second man and Abee nodded. Goji leaned out to get a good whiff of the man.

"You've done this before?" the cobbler said.

The second man looked uncomfortable. He cleared his throat.

"It will work," the second man said. "I start work tomorrow. They're building a new building, but for now we're working just across the road."

"You're going to end up at the end of a noose," the cobbler said.

"Doesn't bother me, brother," the second man said. "The end of life comes one way or another."

The cobbler glared at the second man.

"You're going to screw up my life, Jabez, and I'll hang you myself," the cobbler said.

Unmoved by the cobbler's threat, Jabez simply blinked.

"I did change my name to yours," Jabez said.

"Why?" the cobbler asked.

"I am to be hanged by our father's name," Jabez said.

The cobbler just glared at his brother.

"I knew you wouldn't mind, Oren," Jabez said. "We are both Gowans now."

"I know who you are, Josiah Hughes," the cobbler said, as if the name were an angry threat.

"I know what you did to Daddy, Jonus Gibbons," Jabez said with a sneer.

"That was you!" the cobbler said.

"You're the one who ran away," Jabez said. "And anyway, there's not much of old Josiah left."

Shaking his head at the nonsense, the cobbler gave a frustrated growl. He pointed to the door.

"Get out," the cobbler said. "If I ever see you again, it will be too soon."

Jabez picked up an ornate hat. He straightened his jacket. With a straight back, Jabez Gowans walked out of the cobbler's store and into infamy.

The soft click of the latch was more than the cobbler could stand. He swore. Dropping down, he rested his head in his hands. Time seemed to slow and then freeze. The clock stopped ticking.

Without moving his head, Oren began to speak.

"I know that you are here," Oren Gowans, the cobbler, said.

Abee pointed to herself. Tlanuwa nodded.

"This is the first moment he arrived in Charleston," Oren said. "Soon people began to fall under his control — white men, their women and children, planters, shopkeepers, slaves. I knew it was going to happen. My only chance to kill him was this moment, which is why you are here."

"Thank you," Abee said.

He didn't look up or acknowledge that he'd heard her.

"His body died at the end of a Union Army rope," Oren said. "I survived. I met Ma'am a few years after Charleston fell to the Union Army. I hope this information will in some way pay the debt I owe her."

"She's under his control now," Abee said.

"Yes," Oren said. "It's the only way she can fight him."

"She's fighting him?" The words burst out of her.

"Of course," Oren said. "You see this place?"

"Yes," Abee said.

"He is buried under this building," Oren said. "You will find him here."

As if a bubble burst, time began to move again. The clock began to tick again. The cobbler looked up at the clock and gave a tired sigh. He set his work onto a shelf, grabbed his jacket, and left the shop.

Abee looked at Tlanuwa.

"You should return to the present," Tlanuwa said. "Free the souls on the fields."

"How?" Abee asked.

"Use the Sacred Fire," Tlanuwa said. "You are her master on earth."

"I am?" Abee asked.

"Of course," Tlanuwa said. "The Sacred Fire will cleanse these souls of their enchantment.

Abee gave a nod.

"I will meet you tonight," Tlanuwa said. "We will vanquish this abomination together."

Abee nodded to Tlanuwa. She opened her mouth to respond to him but found herself in the field again. The dust vortex was still whirling on the outer edge of the field.

Grey and white smoke from the Palo Santo bonfires and the sage filled the air.

She took a deep breath and closed her eyes.

"By the Sacred Fire, I release you," Abee whispered.

The souls stopped their labors. They looked around — first at each other and then at Abee — in a kind of stunned awakening. Soon Abee was surrounded by the souls of the trapped.

"Be free," Abee whispered.

En masse, they began to slip away.

Before she did this work, Abee had always imagined that souls would float away to the sky. But in reality, they seemed to just fade away. One woman spirit walked up and knelt down before Abee. Her lips moved.

Abee pressed her ear to see if the blue flame could help her.

"Thank you, daughter," the woman said. "Tell my mother that I love her."

"You are Ma'am's child?" Abee asked.

The woman gave her a slow nod. She reached up to touch Abee's face. Abee felt a tingle of electricity on her face.

"You look so much like her," the woman said. "It gives me great joy to see you, daughter. I always believed that I would see her again. In your face, I have seen my beloved mother once more."

With that, the woman faded away. As if her own mother had died, Abee felt a well of sorrow rise inside. She lowered her head and closed the staff.

The dust vortex ended.

With her head lowered, Abee was standing in the middle of the field, with Goji at her side and Tippi on her shoulder. She felt tears drop from her face into the earth. Wiping her face, she looked up to see that the humans on the edge of the field were cheering and jumping around. A few hugged each other as if they had accomplished a great thing.

Streaked with mud and filthy from the dust, the spiritualist woman testified that the field had been cleared of all evil.

Grinning, Abee started walking to the edge of the field. By the time she'd walked the distance, she felt bone tired. Luckily, Destiny and her mother were standing on the edge. They seemed to be some kind of Charleston royalty, because everyone gave them a wide berth. Destiny hugged Abee. Her mother took one look at Abee.

"That took a lot out of you," Nancy said.

"I'm sorry — I just got so tired," Abee said. "It happens after these things."

"Understandable," Nancy said. "How about we take care of this here and you head home? Can you drive?"

Abee thought for a moment and shook her head.

"I'll take her," Destiny said.

"I have Ma'am," Abee said, gesturing to where Ma'am was sitting.

"I'll help," Nancy said.

Nancy waved. Their cook and Isaiah came over to see what she needed. Soon, Ma'am was carefully eased into the passenger seat of her Chrysler. Abee took the back seat with Goji.

They made it to Destiny's house. With Goji leading the way, they got Ma'am into a comfortable chair in the pool house. Abee fell sound asleep the moment she lay down on the couch.

She dreamed of beautiful plantations filled with laughing people of all colors. The fields were green and growing. No one was enslaved. Instead, they were drawn together out of joy. It was like something in a movie from the 1930s, except the joy was palpable and real. Even in the dream, Abee felt like she was getting a glimpse of a possible heaven.

She opened her eyes in a dark room. The first thing she smelled was herself. Sweat, dirt, and grease clung to her skin and clothes.

"Ugh," she said.

She stumbled to the bathroom, where she took a fast shower. Goji pressed her nose into the curtains of the shower.

"Goji!" Abee said. "I bet you're hungry and need to pee. Give me a second."

Abee finished her shower quickly. Her clothing was so filthy that she grabbed a trash bag and stuck it inside — even her underwear and bra. Luckily, she always brought a back-up bra and plenty of underwear. She dressed in jeans and a long-sleeved T-shirt.

She let Goji out into the fading light of the day to do her business. She turned in place and went to help Ma'am to the toilet. Once on the toilet, Ma'am did her business. Somehow, she knew that was what she was to do. Abee cleaned up Ma'am, settled her back in her chair, and went to look for Tippi. She found the fairy sound asleep, hidden under a blanket shaped like a leaf on the top fold of the couch near where Abee's head had lain.

Goji barked from the backyard, so Abee went to take a look. Isaiah was coming across the lawn with a tray of food. Abee went out to clean up after Goji and followed the houseman into the pool house.

"Gosh, what's all of this?" Abee asked.

"We were waiting and watching for you to wake," Isaiah said. "Destiny said that you eat a lot, so I wanted to get this to you right away. Tiana told me that Destiny said this was your favorite meal."

Isaiah set a tray on the table. Abee looked to see her favorite meal of fried chicken with mashed potatoes and greens on the table. She was instantly starving. She grinned at Isaiah.

"Gordon Johnson is up at the house," Isaiah said. "Along with a few others. They want to thank you for what you did there."

Abee nodded and wondered if it was polite to eat in front of a houseman. Ma'am would know. Her eyes flicked to her great-and-then-some-grandmother.

"I was there, you know," Isaiah said. "I don't have the words to describe what I saw and what I felt."

Abee's full attention returned to the man. His hand was over his heart and his eyes were full of tears.

"That spiritualist went on and on about righting wrongs and freeing those enslaved," Isaiah said. "But I . . . I could feel the release of . . . indescribable suffering, right now, into my bones. It was . . ."

He took a breath and wiped his eyes.

"I can see why you do this work," Isaiah said. "It's so satisfying, or at least it was for me. People were cheering and laughing. I think you're going to have a crowd everywhere you go this week."

His words hit Abee like a ton of bricks. She'd almost forgotten that she had six more plantations to clear before she could go home.

"Well, I know you need your peace and quiet," Isaiah said. "Mr. Beaune asked me to tell you that they would love to see you when you'd like company. He's . . . You know, I think he's going to become mayor after today. I never would have thought it, but after today . . ."

Isaiah nodded and turned to go.

"Just leave the dishes here," Isaiah said. "I'll get them when the cleaning crew comes through."

"Thank you," Abee said. "This house, you, have been such a blessing to me. Thank you."

He grinned and left. Abee closed the door. Turning, she yelped with surprise to find Abraham standing behind her.

"I need to eat," Abee said. "Before anything, I need to eat."

She went around him to the table. Seeing that Isaiah had included a bowl of dog food for Goji, Abee set the bowl on the ground and told Goji to eat. She made sure to set aside two thick chicken legs for Ma'am. She gave Tippi a large piece of the chicken breast. Then, Abee ate everything. She helped Ma'am eat some chicken. When she had finished, she packed up the bones and covered it all with the cover Isaiah had used.

"I need to go up to the house," Abee said to Abraham.

"You *need* to catch this man," Abraham said. "Evil doesn't wait."

"This evil has been waiting a long time," Abee said. "I need to go up there to talk to the people. If I don't, it will just seem plain weird. And what am I going to say?"

She put a big toothy grin on her face.

"I'm off to chase some evil around Charleston," Abee said, while waving her hand like a prom queen.

Abraham grinned, and Abee laughed.

"Business first," Abee said. "When I come back, we'll hunt some *di'mänik*."

"I will stay with my mother," Abraham said with a nod.

"Thank you," Abee said. "I promise, I won't be long. You don't know me, but I'm good at just dropping in and getting away."

Abee grinned, and Abraham smiled.

"By the way, did you have a sister?" Abee asked.

Abraham's whole body clenched as if Abee had caused him instant pain. He gave a quick nod.

"I saw her on the field," Abee said with a smile. "She is at peace now."

Abraham seemed to nearly collapse in relief. He gave Abee a fast nod and turned away. Not one to pick open other people's pain, Abee smiled and left the pool house.

She walked across the grass to the back of the main house. She was about to tap on the door when Tiana opened it. The cook swept Abee into a hug.

"Thank you so much for what you've done," Tiana enthused. "I was so moved and . . . You are truly doing God's work."

Tiana sighed and smiled at Abee.

"Thank you for the chicken," Abee said. "It really hit the spot."

"You are most welcome," Tiana said. "I wasn't sure what dog food to get Goji so I bought her the most expensive."

Tiana lifted her shoulders and grinned.

"Expense account," Tiana said.

Abee grinned.

"Goji ate it down," Abee said. "Thank you."

"She is a beautiful dog," Tiana said. "I was so relieved that you had her with you in the middle of the field. She would protect you and keep you company."

"She's a Goblin hunter," Abee said.

Tiana looked surprised.

"Abee!" Destiny said from the door way.

Abee nodded to Tiana and went to hug Destiny. She had her hand shaken by at least twenty people. Destiny's parents gave her a hug and acted as if she were their longtime family friend. Gordon, the plantation manager for the Beaune Plantation, simply nodded in her direction. His broad smile told her everything she needed to know.

She nodded in return.

She would never remember the names of all of the people. She would certainly remember how elated they were. Desmond was working the room. She saw a small woman in the corner accepting checks, likely for Destiny's father's campaign.

After an hour, Abee made her excuses and left.

She was just walking across the grass when Tiana ran out. She gave Abee a paper bag and ran back toward the house. Abee opened the bag to find two roast-beef sandwiches, carrots, and at least twenty tiny cinnamon sugar cookies.

"In case you get hungry later," Tiana said before she went inside.

Abee waved in thanks, but Tiana was gone. Abee walked back to the pool house. Goji got up to greet her but was so exhausted from the day that she went to lie down again. Tippi was sitting on Ma'am's leg. Abraham was standing in front of Ma'am.

"How's it going?" Abee asked no one in particular.

"There's a man . . ." Abraham started.

Tlanuwa poked his head out from the kitchen.

"Are we ready?" Tlanuwa asked, impatiently.

"Uh, what's going on?" Abee asked the priest.

"I have been arguing with this . . ." Tlanuwa said. He glared at Abraham.

"I don't trust him," Abraham said. "He's got that look."

"I look like a person who is native to this place," Tlanuwa said, as if making a point.

"That's the problem," Abraham said. "I don't want his kind . . ."

"Whoa, no racism," Abee said. "Tlanuwa is dedicated to the Sacred Fire, which I am entrusted with on Earth. He is here to help me, to teach me how to use the Sacred Fire."

"Sacred fire?" Abraham asked.

Abee touched her chest, and her entire body was covered in blue fire. Abraham jerked back.

"It won't hurt you," Abee said.

"It's . . ." Abraham looked at Abee and then looked at Ma'am. "Powerful?"

Abee nodded.

"Tlanuwa says that it will destroy the *dí'mänik*," Abee said.

"*Dí'mänik?*" Abraham asked.

"That's what Tippi . . ." Abee sighed and gestured to the tiny fairy. Tippi waved at the spirit. " . . . called the being inside the man," Abee said with a sigh. "The evil power that . . ."

Abee rubbed the bridge of her nose in exhaustion and frustration. When she looked up at Abraham, he was grinning at her. He nodded to Ma'am and back at Abee. Clearly that gesture was something Ma'am did way back in the 1800s. Abee gave a rueful shake of her head.

"We need to work together," Abee said. "That's the point."

"I am not sure why we need this spirit," Tlanuwa sniffed.

"Because Ma'am wants me to," Abee said.

"She told you this," Tlanuwa said.

"No, she can't," Abee said. "I can just feel it. Abraham is here for a reason. We will need him before the end."

Tlanuwa looked at Abraham. The way Abraham glumly looked at Tlanuwa, Abee wondered if he might actually be younger than she'd thought.

"Alright," Abee looked at Tlanuwa. "Do we need to go to the origin or . . ."

"We cannot change what has happened," Tlanuwa said. He nodded to Abraham. "I am sorry for that. I would rather free these people from this man. But the past is done. Written in stone. We can go back to view it, but we cannot change it."

"How was the cobbler able to talk to us?" Abee asked.

"It's a bubble in time," Tlanuwa said. "Something your Ma'am did. She seems to have known that the day would come when you would free the world from this creature. She left this bubble in time for you to find when you went looking."

"She used to talk about it," Abraham said. "Her daughter who would destroy the creature."

"I imagine she didn't think it would take this long," Tlanuwa said.

Abee nodded rather than respond.

"To answer your original question, I am not sure what we need to do," Tlanuwa said.

"I have an idea," Abee said. "Ma'am and I have been working on something . . ."

Tlanuwa and Abraham looked at Abee. Tippi flew up to Abee's shoulder. Goji got up to stand at her side. Abee grinned at the men.

She opened her hand, and the piece of staff appeared. It grew into her usual staff. She took one end and pulled on it. A blue-flame thong appeared. In minutes, she was holding a blue-flame stock whip with a three-inch staff with a six-foot blue-flame thong on the end.

"Goji got a scent of the man when we went back," Abee said. "Didn't you, Goji?"

The dog looked up at Goji. Abee touched Goji and she was covered in a coat of blue flame. She touched Tippi- and the fairy was protected.

"Abraham?" Abee asked.

"I will protect him," Tlanuwa said.

"How . . .?" Abraham asked.

"He is made of the Sacred Flame," Abee said. "Come on. Let's hunt some *di'mänik*. Tlanuwa?"

"Abee," Tlanuwa said.

"Can you open a portal of time?" Abee asked.

"Of course," Tlanuwa said.

A giant hole appeared in the tile floor. Abee gestured to Abraham.

"Follow us," Abee said. "If you feel like you cannot keep up, grab hold of me. Goji?"

The dog looked up at her.

"Find the *di'mänik*," Abee said.

Goji gave a single bark and jumped into the hole. Tippi flew off Abee's shoulder. The tiny fairy landed on Goji's collar just as they entered the hole.

"How does she . . ." Abraham said.

"She's a Goblin hunter," Abee said. "As long as she knows what she's looking for, she'll find it."

"And does she know?" Abraham asked.

Abee nodded.

"Now we follow," Abee said.

She stepped into the hole. Inside the realm of time, she saw thick, tan-colored ribbons that seemed to go everywhere. In some places, the ribbon folded back on itself. In others, it was tied in a knot. She saw places where someone or something had pinned the time so that everything at that moment stayed in place.

For a moment, Abee stood in place to get her bearings. Hearing Goji bark, Abee lit the other end of her staff with the blue flame and ran in the direction of her dog's bark. She felt more than saw Tlanuwa and Abraham following her close behind. They ran until they were out of breath, but the dog was moving too fast.

Tlanuwa gestured to Abee's staff. Abee raised the staff over her head and flicked the blue flame whip. The end of the whip wrapped around Goji's collar.

"Hang on!" Abee said.

Tlanuwa and Abraham grabbed onto Abee. They flew through the realm of time. Somewhere up ahead, Goji stopped running. They flew to her. Tlanuwa used his skill to slow and then stop their momentum. They dropped where Goji was standing.

Goji lifted her nose and made a loud, baying bark.

"Goji says he's here," Abee said. "How do we . . .?"

They were standing in the middle of what had been a road. The moon cast the dirt road in an eerie light. The buildings on either side of the road were in rubble. What remained of Oren Gowan's cobbler's shop was on their right.

Nothing stirred. Somewhere off in the distance, they could hear the boom of cannons. There was a kind of unnerving, still silence that sent shivers up Abee's spine.

An older man and a younger man appeared at the end of the road with a heavily laden cart. The cart seemed heavy. As the men approached, they could see that the cart was laden with dead bodies. The men came up to where the cobbler shop had stood.

"This is the address," the older man said.

"There's no one here," the younger man said.

The older man lifted a shoulder in a shrug.

"Probably for the best," the younger man said.

They rolled a man's body off the pile. The body landed in a thud on the ground. The younger man took a shovel from the cart and began digging. The younger man barely scratched the surface of the earth before the men rolled the body into the hole. The older man helped the younger man pile the dirt and rubble over the body. They stowed the shovel before wheeling the cart down the road.

"Now what?" Abraham asked.

"One moment, young man," Tlanuwa said.

As if called by his words, the spirit of Jonus Gibbons rose above the shop. Before he could speak, Abee lashed out with her blue-flame whip. The end of the whip wrapped around Gibbons' ankle. The creature screamed and called.

He tried to speak, but Tlanuwa threw a blue-flame gag over his mouth.

In minutes, the *dí'mänik* cast off the spirit of Jonus Gibbons. The spirit fell away, and the *dí'mänik* rose.

Abee acted without hesitation. She lashed at the *dí'mänik* with her blue-flame whip. She managed to catch both of the creature's feet. The creature screamed in desperate pain as the whip wrapped around its ankles.

To Abee's surprise, Ma'am appeared — or, rather, a form of her Ma'am appeared. She was either an apparition or possibly an astral projection. Abee would take Ma'am help in any form.

"Hold on!" Ma'am said. She pointed to Abraham. "Take the wooden part of the whip. Don't touch the flame."

"Yes, Mother," Abraham said.

Abee passed him the whip. She automatically made another. Ma'am nodded to Abee. She lashed the *dí'mänik* around the waist. Tlanuwa followed suit by lashing his hands with tendrils of blue flame that came from the palms of his hands.

The three of them held the creature in the blue flame, like cowboys holding a wild bull. The *dí'mänik* bucked and writhed. The creature fought with all its might to get away. They held it fast.

It was only then that Abee saw that Ma'am had bound the creature's mouth to keep him from calling for help or working magic.

The Mother of the Sacred Flame appeared.

Abee could never be certain of what happened next. What she remembered was the Mother consuming the demon in brilliant blue flame, but only after Ma'am had grown to nearly nine feet. There was something about the plantations and the burning of Charleston, but, mostly, it was a blur. Abee awoke on the pool house couch at dawn in modern-day Charleston.

Her first thought was Ma'am. She sat up. The chair she'd left her Ma'am sitting in was empty. Panicked, she jumped up and pulled some clothing on. She was standing at the door when she heard Ma'am calling her.

Abee stumbled toward the sound and wound up in the bedroom of the small pool house.

Ma'am was lying on the bed. She was wearing her bed clothing. The covers were rumpled in such a way as to indicate that she'd been there all night.

Abee put her hand to her mouth to keep from weeping at the sight.

"Abee?" Ma'am asked.

Ma'am gave her a soft smile.

"Back to sleep with you," Ma'am said. "I thought we could take the long way home. I don't feel well, so you'll need to drive."

"Cancel the rest of the week?" Abee asked.

"Those plantations are cleared of spirits now," Ma'am said.

"Really?" Abee asked.

Ma'am gave her a quick nod. She waved Abee out of the bedroom.

Abee stumbled back to the couch. She sat up for a while before sheer exhaustion overwhelmed her. She lay down in her street clothing.

"You did really good, Abee," Ma'am said from the bedroom. "I'm proud of you."

"I met your son," Abee said. "Abraham."

Ma'am didn't answer.

"Your daughter told me to tell you that she loved you," Abee said.

Abee could tell from Ma'am's breathing that her *truly great* grandmother was crying. Smiling to herself, she fell into a dreamless sleep.

LIKE THIS BOOK?

Take a moment to leave a review. Even a few words or a sentence can be the difference of a book rising in popularity or being lost in the bowels of your favorite bookseller.

Claudia Hall Christian writes great stories about good people caught in difficult times. She is the author of the *Alex the Fey* thrillers, the longest running serial fiction — the *Denver Cereal*, the *Seth and Ava Mysteries*, as well as *Suffer a Witch* and the *Queen of Cool*. She is the founder of Women and Fiction and runs the Everyday Kindness project. She keeps bees and Plott Hounds in Denver, Colorado where she lives with her husband.

You can find Claudia at her website: ClaudiaHallChristian.com Claudia is active on social media at Twitter, Facebook, and Instagram.

StoriesbyClaudia.com is a website where you can read Claudia's work and get information about her Book Club. The Abee Normal novellas will continue.